EASY TARGET

By Cynthia Wall, KA7ITT

Best Wishes,
Cynthia Wall
KA7ITT

**Published by the
American Radio Relay League
Newington, CT USA 06111**

Cover and illustrations by Sheila Dianne Somerville

For my husband,
Dave,
Who cares for all the creatures of the sea

CONTENTS

The Congress finds that —

(1) Certain species and population stocks of marine mammals are, or may be, in danger of extinction or depletion as a result of man's activities;

(6) Marine mammals have proven themselves to be resources of great international significance, esthetic and recreational as well as economic, and it is the sense of the Congress that they should be protected and encouraged to develop to the greatest extent feasible commensurate with sound policies of resource management...

From the U.S. Marine Mammal Protection Act 1972

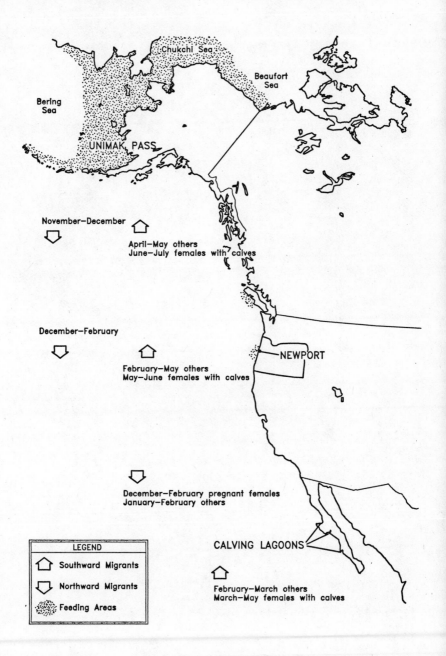

Chapter 1

Homeward Bound

Wednesday, April 17th, 11 a.m.
San Diego, California

"Look!" the young girl yelled. The captain of the tourist whale-watching boat *Sea Witch*, from San Diego, turned to look at his youngest passenger, eight-year-old Jessica. Her face, rosy from excitement and the chill March air, peeked out from a warm-hooded coat. "Look!" she shouted again. "A mama whale and a baby!"

Captain Bill Weinstock's eyes followed the direction of her small finger. After ten years in the whale-watching charter business, he could often spot the migrating animals before anyone else even suspected they were there. But, he gladly gave over the thrill of being the first to see one of the huge mammals to this young passenger who was now clutching her mother's hand and jumping up and down.

"Good for you!" he exclaimed enthusiastically. "It's a gray all right with a baby working hard to keep up. They've got a long trip ahead of them. About 4500 more miles to go before they're home. Look closely, everyone; there may be more around."

Just then, someone on the other side of the boat yelled. A surfacing whale had spouted explosively less than one-hundred yards off the port side.

"They usually travel in groups," Captain Weinstock explained. "But going home, they tend to be a lot more spread out. Plus, they're going about half speed so the babies can keep up. In December, when they're on their way to the breeding and birthing lagoons, they come roaring — well, roaring for them — through here at about five miles an hour. Now they're slowed to two and a half."

Jessica shrieked with delight as the baby whale surfaced briefly and the wet shine of his perfect young body shimmered in the morning sunlight.

"I'm going to name him Silver Star," she said. "Here Silver Star, here Silver Star," she called and then laughed as the tails of the two whales, one huge and one small, disappeared under the surface of the Pacific Ocean.

Two-month-old, "Silver Star," heard the girl's voice. It added to the other sounds flooding his hearing senses — the lap of the waves, the low communicative groans from his mother, the muscular thrusts of her huge body.

Sound was only one of the ocean's wonders the young whale was experiencing. Keeping his mother in close sight, he was still able to watch the life around them in the vibrant sea. There was so much to see, to hear, to feel, to smell and taste. His brain was filled with the newness of his life and the sensory experiences cascading over him. His form was growing in size and strength every day, and he easily imitated his mother's flowing dolphin motion as he followed her north.

The water near San Diego was dark, murky blue-gray and as Silver Star looked down, there was no friendly shadow following him. One of his earliest memories was of his own shadow on the floor of shallow sunlit Scammon's Lagoon in Baja California, where he had been born. Once the site of bloody whaling harvests, Scammon's was now a protected sanctuary for the birth of the baby grays.

"Wow!" said Jessica to her mother as Silver Star surfaced once again. "That's a big baby!"

"Two thousand pounds and fourteen feet at birth," Captain Weinstock told her. "And now he's even bigger. You know how the milk you drink is one percent or two percent fat?"

Jessica nodded.

"Well, whale's milk is forty percent fat. That baby is gaining fifty pounds a day."

"I weigh fifty-five!"

The captain patted her on the head.

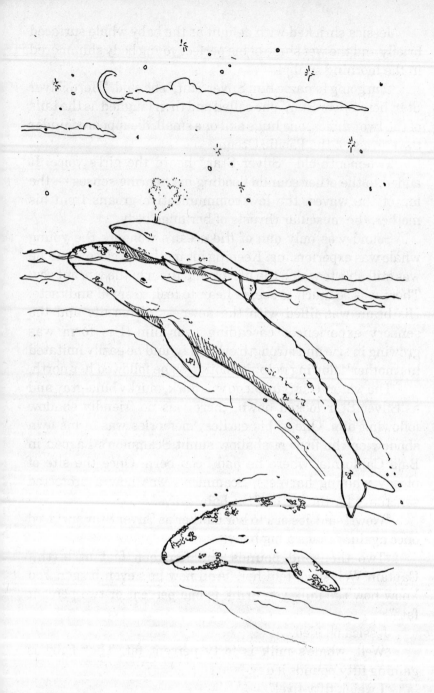

"Then you're just a little bigger than one day in a baby whale's life."

She laughed as the whales disappeared under the surface again.

Silver Star swam hard to keep up. This was very different from his early days filled with peaceful cycles of eating, caresses from his mother, and sleeping under her watchful guardianship.

Warm days when he swam briefly away from his mother but always hastened back when she called him. Days with other young whales. Most had been born before he was, and as they grew to traveling weight and strength, he watched as they left the peaceful lagoon behind their mothers.

Then one day in late March, his mother swam purposefully through the narrow tidal channels of the lagoon toward the open sea.

Silver Star followed her closely, letting the current from her powerful tail carry him. Close by, "Moon," an aging, scarred female whale trailed them out of the cove. There had been no babies for Moon in years.

As the cooler water of the Pacific hit Moon, it was tempting to turn back to the safe, warm lagoon. The migration back home would take a terrible toll on her weakening body. She had already depleted most of her fat stores, but her determination to return to the rich Arctic Sea was fierce as she forced her body to keep up with Silver Star and his mother.

"A third one!" Jessica exclaimed happily as everyone applauded the appearance of a huge whale off the port side.

Captain Weinstock lowered his binoculars.

"Well, I'll be — I think it's Moon. A fisherman out of San Pedro named her about 20 years ago. She's been spotted up and down the coast almost every year. Nobody knows if that crescent-shaped scar near her blowhole is from a shark or a harpoon. Wonder how old she is now — must be getting up there. Hope she makes it."

"I bet that's Silver Star's grandma," Jessica said.

Captain Weinstock smiled at her and then pointed at all three whales. They had changed course slightly and were now heading at an angle out to sea away from the boat.

"There they go," he said. "Bon Voyage."

"Have a good trip, Silver Star!" Jessica yelled to the wake created by the whales' powerful ten-foot-wide tails.

Beneath the ocean surface, the trio set their course due north. The noise of the surf on their right would guide the two females. Silver Star would follow them trustingly. His young mind could not know of the 5000 mile trip that had brought his mother and the others to Baja. The trip that started last fall in Siberia through the Chukchi Sea to the Bering Strait just ahead of bitter storms and increasing ice cover. Then through the Bering Sea southward.

He had no memory of his pre-birth life. He couldn't know that as he had stirred within his mother, she swam all night toward the Umiak Pass, the first break in the Aleutian Island chain. He had not yet heard the clicks of killer whales or tasted the waters pouring from Canadian rivers.

All of this plus the sea otter colonies of Monterey, the kelp beds of Morro Bay, the warm waters near Point Conception, the thousands of people along shore watching their migration were knowledge to the two females — all of this and more awaited him on the return journey.

But something new was being added to their migratory journey this year. A lumber freighter named the *Si Maria* from Colombia, South America, was already underway on a second spring voyage up the Pacific Coast. Its declared cargo: exotic South American hardwoods — its real cargo: cocaine.

On the day that Silver Star and his mother and Moon passed by San Diego, the *Si Maria* was one thousand miles south of them. The whales had no way of knowing that in the weeks to come, the plodding freighter with its lilting Spanish name would come between them and survival. And even if they could know, they would be powerless to prevent the encounter.

Chapter 2

Stormy Nights

Thursday, April 18th, 11 p.m.
Newport, Oregon

"Y ou sure you don't want to come back with us?"
Megan asked Kim. Kim shook her head at her
companions. The four girls, all spring-term
residents at the Oregon State University Marine Science
Center sat enjoying a late night cup of hot chocolate in a small
cafe in Newport Harbor's Old Town. Outside the fogged-up
windows, a fierce spring storm raged. Even though they were
at the far end of Yaquina Bay, the girls could still hear the roll
of pounding surf on the other side of the jetties.

Megan, Julia, and Tracie stood up, glancing at the wall
clock which read 11 p.m. Tracie put her hand out to touch
Kim's arm when she didn't get up with them.

"What's the matter, Kim?"

"Oh, just boyfriend problems, or rather lack of boyfriend
problems," Kim smiled ruefully.

"So that's why you're so quiet tonight," Julia said.

"Yeah, I guess I've been doing too much thinking today,"
Kim said softly.

"Want to talk about it?" Tracie asked.

"Not really."

"Well, why don't you follow us back to the Marine Science
Center? I know you've got your car here since you came down
early to buy supplies, but I'd just feel better if we all went back
at the same time."

Again, Kim shook her head.

"What are you going to do anyway?" Julia asked.

"Just walk around the harbor for awhile. Don't worry, I
promise I won't be long. I just like to walk on stormy nights.

Half hour max, I promise. Besides, you know I always carry my trusty radio with me."

The girls laughed. Kim and her ham radio. They had watched curiously two weeks ago when Kim arrived with her belongings. Sure, she had the usual assortment of books, stuffed animals, CDs, and other college fare, but Kim had also carried in three cartons of Amateur Radio gear. Politely, she'd asked Julia and Megan, her roommates in the compact dorm apartment if there was a corner of a table she could use. She was delighted to find that the two of them had opted to give her the small single bedroom in the two-bedroom apartment. She had never dreamed she would have a room to herself.

The girls had been fascinated, as Kim strung an all-band dipole antenna out the window to the corner of another building — with just a little help from Dan Millenton, a graduate student whose room adjoined the desired corner.

"I've roomed with someone who practiced flute all night, with a marble sculptor, with a girl who decorated cakes for every occasion — but never with a Samuel, excuse me Samantha Morse," laughed Julia. "This is great — what happens now?"

Kim showed them what happened next when she got the transceiver tuned up. After a short test transmission with a ham in California, she gave her first CQ call. The girls' mouths opened wide when the first answer to that call was a Japanese student at the University of Tokyo.

So now, when Kim waved her small handheld two-meter radio at them — the one she was able to talk to local operators on — they smiled again, but that didn't keep them from worrying. Kim didn't talk much about her personal life, but they gathered from what she did say that she had broken up with her longtime boyfriend, Marc. In fact, Kim had even hinted that the breakup was one reason why she had chosen to spend her spring term away from the Corvallis campus.

Megan tried once again to get Kim to drive home behind them.

"Really," Kim insisted. "This isn't the New York waterfront or something. I just want to walk alone a little bit.

This is one of my favorite places. I think better when I'm around ships. Kind of like I can will my thoughts to go the places the ships have been and bring me back wisdom."

"You're weird, Kim," Megan laughed. "These are mostly fishing trawlers, not exotic yachts, and most of them haven't been much beyond the fishing grounds just outside the bay."

Kim smiled. The girls reluctantly left her after she promised to start home within the hour. They got in Megan's elderly Ford and honked good-bye to Kim as she bent her head against the wind and walked down the sidewalk in front of the tourist shops. Only one or two of the restaurants were open at this hour, and even these were mostly vacant.

The rain had stopped and Kim looked up to see a moment of moonlight between the heavy clouds being driven inland by the storm's winds. She took a deep breath and tried to relax her shoulders. She liked the girls and all, but by nature she was a solitary person. Her last summer as a fire lookout had proven that.

She'd been grateful last fall that she'd gotten into the college dorm that was all single rooms. She just found that having time alone made it easier to study. If she needed to work all night on a paper (or spend the night talking to foreign stations by ham radio!) she needn't worry about keeping her roommates awake.

Winter term had brought a major change in her life. Marc had pressed for a commitment from her — a promise that they would be more than just special friends — that they would pledge themselves to each other to eventually marry. The request had taken Kim by surprise. There wasn't anyone she cared for more than Marc, but did she love him enough to promise herself to him forever?

She begged him to give her time to think. She couldn't answer him the next day nor the next week. And Marc interpreted that as a rejection. To Kim's surprise, he became sullen and stopped calling her. She wrote him a letter, asking if they couldn't be "just friends" and let other more serious matters wait until they graduated.

"If you have to think about it, Kim, then I guess your answer is no," he said one day when he finally called after receiving her letter. "I think it's best if we stop seeing each other."

"Are you sure about that?" Kim asked tearfully.

"I'm sure," Marc replied quietly.

The next few weeks had been terrible. When she did see Marc on campus, he ignored her. She felt physically ill — unable to eat or sleep. Her zoology professor, Dr. Mary Hitham, noticed the change in her. Kim worked as her office helper two afternoons a week. Grateful for the friendly ear, Kim blurted out all her troubles.

"Kim, I don't know if you'd be interested, but there's a vacancy over at the Marine Science Center next term. You've expressed an interest in marine biology — maybe this would be a good way to find out if that should be your major. Dr. Bolny will be there most of the term before he heads back to the Arctic for more research, and you know his reputation."

Indeed, Kim did. Dr. Frank Bolny was considered one of the top whale physiologists in the world. The chance to work with him might be a chance she would never have again. Kim accepted the offer.

Over spring vacation, she busied herself getting ready for her term at the coast. Her parents had been relieved to see her smiling once again and speaking optimistically of the future. They were both very fond of Marc, but Mr. and Mrs. Stafford were too wise to ask many questions.

"If she wants to tell us what happened, she will," Mrs. Stafford told her husband late one night after Kim had gone to bed. "Marc should know by now that you can't pressure Kim into anything she doesn't want to do. I just don't think she feels she's lived enough to make a decision like that."

Those were Kim's sentiments exactly as she walked alone on the pier between salmon and crab processing plants. The wind buffeted the fishing boats tied to docks below the pier. Kim listened to the creaking of rigging and the flapping of canvas. A solitary gull hung motionless in the wind, fighting its way back to a nighttime roosting place.

Kim fingered the two-meter radio in the deep pocket of her denim pants. She missed saying goodnight to Marc by ham radio. Whether he was at his home in Portland and she in hers in Salem or whether they were just a block apart on the OSU campus, they always talked for a few minutes every night.

She wiped moisture from her cheeks. Was it starting to rain again? No, not yet. *Just me,* she thought sadly. She leaned against the side of a building, somewhat sheltered from the wind and watched the waves tossing moonlit foam in the bay.

"KA7SJP monitoring," Kim said softly into her radio's microphone. She doubted anyone would be on frequency at this hour, but it never hurt to try. More than once, a conversation with a stranger had cheered her. After all, that was how she had met Marc! Another wave of remembering swept over her but was interrupted by a low male voice.

"KA7SJP, this is N6GP at the Newport Coast Guard Station. Name's Gary. Good evening."

Kim felt her spirits lift. "N6GP from KA7SJP. Good Evening. Name's Kim. I'm a resident student at the Marine Science Center for the spring term. I'm surprised to hear anyone on at this hour."

"Glad to meet you, Kim. I'm on the night watch here at the station. I leave my two-meter rig on — usually stormy nights are pretty slow here. Most ships are smart enough to stay out of the way of the storm. But occasionally, we hear someone in trouble."

They chatted for several minutes until Gary said he had a phone call. He signed off by inviting Kim to stop by the station someday to say hello in person.

"I'd enjoy that, Gary. Thank you. KA7SJP clear."

Kim tucked the radio in her pocket and started walking back down the pier toward the street. The QSO (conversation) with Gary made her feel better than she had in several weeks. Rain began falling, first with occasional drops and then in earnest. Kim ran, pulling her hood forward to shield her face. She reached the sidewalk and turned left toward her car parked down by the cafe. Now the lights were off in all the businesses except for the Pelican Bar next to the cafe.

Judging from the noise inside, more than one local was spending the evening celebrating the storm with alcohol. She stopped abruptly as three men came jostling out the door. They were arguing violently, and Kim shrank back into the shadows of the building, afraid to pass them.

One of them was dressed in Army fatigues; the other two had on dark-colored thick woolen overshirts and jeans. They were obviously drunk and angry about something. Kim glanced anxiously across the street, wondering if she could cross over without being noticed and circumvent them to get to her car.

"I say we go tonight — get it and take it to Spokane. Then, we'll have a couple of weeks free until the next load," one of the men yelled at the other who gave him a shove as an answer.

"The stuff's not going anywhere," the man in fatigues said quietly. He appeared to be sober in contrast to the other two. "Let's wait until the storm dies down — we almost got killed on that last one. Besides," he said, turning to the others, "neither of you is in any shape to do anything but sleep now."

"Whadya mean? I'm fine," one of them growled.

They started to walk unevenly down the sidewalk, and Kim took this as her opportunity to dart across the street. Quickly, she ran down the sidewalk and back across the street to her car. She had her key out in her hand, but in the darkness, she fumbled for the keyhole. She tried to look calm as the men lurched their way toward her. Apparently, theirs was the pickup truck parked ahead of her car.

Kim glanced at the truck out of the corner of her eye as she jammed the key into the door lock. A small Zodiac runabout poked out through the open truck canopy door. One corner of her brain registered the fact that it really wasn't very good weather to be out in a small boat, but just then, she finally got the car door open. She slid in the car and was pulling the door shut when a strong hand grabbed it.

Terrified, Kim looked up to see the face of one of the men. He was unshaven and the sour odor of alcohol permeated the air.

"Hey, where you going, girl? How about some fun?"

He gave Kim's long ponytail a yank as he turned to grin back at his companions. Kim slammed the door shut and snapped the lock. Shaking, she put the key in the ignition and turned on the headlights. Everything seemed to be in slow motion as she struggled to put the car in reverse. The three men were right in front of her headlights, checking something in the back of the truck. The man who had grabbed her door thumped his hand down on her car's hood. Kim backed up hastily and to her surprise, the same man grinned at her and waved.

Just a bunch of drunks having fun, she told herself as she pulled out in the street and drove past them. One last glance as she went by the man in fatigues bending over to pick something up from the street. The wind flipped his shirt up and for a brief second, Kim was sure she saw a handgun tucked in the waistband of his pants.

Still shaking from the encounter, Kim made her way up the hill leading to the Coast Highway. With an eye on her rearview mirror, she put the car in fourth and pushed down the gas pedal. She was halfway across the bridge spanning the bay when she saw bright headlights coming up on her fast.

"No," she whispered, pushing the pedal to the floor. In the heavy rain, she could barely see, and the bright lights shining into her rearview mirror were blinding her. Desperately, she reached up and pointed the mirror down. Her brain raced, trying to decide what to do.

Just beyond the bridge was the turn to the Marine Science Center. Trying to make the sharp corner, she skidded on the slick pavement barely missing the concrete bridge pillar. She looked in the mirror and froze. The truck was bearing down on her.

Chapter 3

Mysterious Deaths

Thursday, April 18th, midnight
Newport, Oregon

With the men pursuing her, Kim sped down the road, spraying gravel in all directions. Could she get her handheld radio out of her pocket? No, it took all of her concentration just to keep the car on the road. She roared into the Marine Science Center parking lot and blasted the horn, not daring to stop the car.

Oh come on, somebody, help! she prayed silently.

But then as suddenly as the men had appeared, they were gone. Tires squealing on the wet pavement, they turned their truck 180 degrees and raced back down the access road that led up to Highway 101.

Kim collapsed limply over the steering wheel. No one had heard her honking. The Marine Science Center was dark and except for entryway lights in the student housing section, it looked like everyone was sleeping. She pulled her radio from her pocket and considered calling Gary at the Coast Guard Station. But the men really seemed to have left. Sobbing with relief, Kim parked her car next to the building and ran through the beating rain to the student apartments at the back. She let herself in and locked the door behind her.

Megan was the only one awake when Kim tiptoed in. She heard Kim gasping for breath and came to the door of her bedroom.

"Kim, are you okay? What happened?" she asked, alarmed by her roommate's tear-streaked face.

It was a minute before Kim could get any words out.

"Oh just some real creeps — drunks I guess. They followed me, but they're gone. I'm okay now, really I am," said Kim sinking onto her bed.

"I knew you should have come home with us."

"Probably so," Kim agreed ruefully. "Next time, I won't be so headstrong."

"Can I get you anything?"

"No, I'm fine really — just need to relax and get to bed."

"Promise to tell me the details in the morning?" Megan said, still looking worried. "I've got an early call in the morning to help Dr. Bolny."

"Sure, Megan. And thanks."

Kim lay down on her bed fully clothed and waited for her heart to quit pounding. Gradually, she began to stop shaking. She got up quietly and went in the bathroom to brush her teeth and wash her face.

One a.m. — her bedside clock glowed cheerfully in the dark.

And I'm supposed to be up at six too, Kim thought wearily. *Next time I need to do some thinking, I'll do it in the afternoon.*

She pulled the covers up over her shoulders and closed her eyes.

* * *

"Well, look at Little Miss Ponytail run," George laughed as their pickup slid sideways turning out of the parking lot.

"Why leave? She might have been fun!" Les, the drunken man in fatigues complained.

"You're so sloshed you can't see. Didn't you notice her license plate — KA something? She's a radio operator — probably calling the police on us right now."

"Supposin' she got ours?"

"I doubt it — she was ahead of us. We can change them to be safe. Besides, after we pick up those last bundles, we've got a week free — don't know about you guys, but once we get paid, I'd like to do a little high living — none of this living in cheap motels bit like we're doing now. And I'd like to see some sunshine too. This has been a long two months carting that stuff everywhere."

There was a grunt of approval from Les and a loud snore from Dirk, the third man. George resumed normal speed as he hit Highway 101 and headed south toward the Sea Urchin Motel. Half of the lights were burned out on the weather-beaten six-unit structure that faced east away from the ocean.

No view, very little heat, but the price was right — $22 a night. Actually, they had plenty of money to stay in the fanciest place in town, but George felt they might attract too much attention. He parked the truck in back under a clump of shore pines.

"Beddy bye time boys," he snickered as he opened the door to let the fresh sea air scour out the beer fumes within the truck cab.

Les jabbed an elbow into Dirk's ribs who came awake spouting profanity.

"Shut up!" George ordered him in a whisper. "Let's not advertise that we're back."

* * *

Friday, April 19th, 7 a.m.
Newport, Oregon

Kim woke up to the happy chatter of her roommates as they prepared for breakfast.

"So what was all that about last night?" Megan questioned her.

Kim sat up and rubbed her eyes. In the warm security of morning and her friends, last night seemed like just a bad dream.

"Oh, I'm not sure it was anything. As I was getting into my car, some drunks came out of a bar and one of them tried to grab my hair. I got in the car and thought that was all there was to it, until their headlights blinded me in the rearview mirror. They actually chased me into the parking lot, but then they left. I was pretty scared at the time, but in the light of morning, I guess they were just out having fun."

"Did you get their license plate?"

"No, it was dark and raining and they were behind me. A blue pickup — American model. Standard size and kind of beat up so it was probably pretty old. That's all I could tell for sure."

"The next time we tell you to come home with us, you'd better do it," Julia lectured.

"Yes, mother."

The girls giggled as they got dressed. Julia was the first into their small apartment kitchen, and she pulled a box of dry cereal from the cupboard. The girls laughed again as Kim made herself a steaming bowl of oatmeal and put some raisins and honey on it.

"Yeah, yeah, we know — a day without oatmeal is a day without sunshine," Megan said. "But every day?"

They chatted amicably as they ate and then grabbed their notebooks to attend a lecture by Dr. Bolny. Normally, the students' days were spent in the labs doing everything from dissecting dead marine mammals to monitoring signals from satellites that tracked whales.

Today, however, Dr. Bolny was giving a lecture to the resident students plus a group of marine biology students who had driven over from the OSU campus. The topic: whale strandings.

Whenever and wherever whales stranded themselves, singly or in groups, Dr. Bolny was one of the first persons to be called. His expertise in returning the giant mammals to the sea had undoubtedly saved many lives. Photos of whales lying on beaches, dying from heat prostration and the weight of their own bodies, brought sympathetic murmurs from the young audience.

"We're still not sure what causes the strandings in many cases," Dr. Bolny told them. "It may be disease or a case of follow the leader. All the strandings that have occurred have been in toothed whales such as these photos of sperm whales taken in Florence. The animals are highly social and if some of them come ashore, the others follow."

"You say they're always toothed whales?" a young man in the back of the room questioned. "What about the gray whale found in December down by Brookings and the other one up at Seaside earlier?"

Dr. Bolny paused and scratched his head.

"I was just getting to that. Just a minute while I change the slide carousel."

There were some whispered comments as he readjusted the focus on the projector and brought the first slide into clear view. The students gasped when they realized what they were looking at. A badly decomposed fifty-foot gray whale lay on the beach. Part of its right side behind the head looked like a huge bite had been taken out of it. A man in the photo was measuring the gaping hole.

"We don't call this an official stranding. The whale was dead when it washed ashore. And we wouldn't think too much about it at all except that as you just mentioned there was another case at Seaside. Actually there were two others found down near San Diego. All of them were males — almost certainly returning to Baja on their migration from Alaska."

"Do white sharks attack whales?"

"Not usually unless the whale is injured or sick. Of course, a dead whale is target for all the scavengers of the ocean. Three of these animals appear to have the distinctive bites of white sharks. One whale was so decomposed, it was hard to tell anything. We don't know if there is some viral illness attacking them or whether this is just coincidence."

There were further speculations from the students and Dr. Bolny listened and responded to each.

"Obviously, this could be very serious. The grays were hunted almost to extinction by the early 1900's. In fact by the mid 1940's, only 8,000 to 10,000 gray whales existed. Thanks to the Marine Mammal Protection Act of the 70's and their being listed as an endangered species, we have almost 21,000 now. In fact, they've recovered to the point that they've been removed from the endangered species list. What a tragedy it will be if their numbers start to decline again."

"Has anyone dissected a body?"

Dr. Bolny actually laughed.

"That would be quite a chore. By the time they've washed ashore, they're in such bad shape, the Health Department is anxious for them to be buried with a backhoe. A dead whale isn't something you want to keep around for a long time. But where there has been viable tissue left, we've taken samples. To my knowledge, nothing unusual has shown up."

At the break, Kim and her roommates discussed the dead whales. All of them had assisted as official whale watchers over spring break, and they felt a close kinship to the magnificent animals who traveled so far every year.

"I hope none of the mothers and babies die," Julia said.

"I believe so far the counts taken around San Diego have been normal," Kim said. "Anyway, that's what I heard Dr. Bolny tell someone in the hall."

"**Remember, their northward migration is just beginning,**" Julia said. "There have only been a few seen up this far. I bet we won't know for a couple of years if this is just a fluke or a trend."

"Wouldn't it be terrible if there were some disease that actually wiped out an entire species? I can't imagine the world without gray whales," Megan added, shaking her head sadly.

"The whaling industry almost did just that," Joel, a fellow student at the next table commented. "Our Earth's balance certainly is fragile. I think the most important thing I've learned here is how incredible it is that we humans continue to take our planet for granted."

The students returned to the lecture hall in a somber mood.

Chapter 4

Easy Target

Saturday, April 20th, 1 a.m.
Just north of San Diego

At midnight on April 20th, Freddie Vasquez, a.k.a. Fred Walner, walked restlessly up and down the decks of the *Si Maria*. Something told him they were definitely in whale country. Although they'd seen a few grays near Baja, the only ones that had come close to the ship had been during the daylight hours.

Passing the many lagoons near Guerrero Negro, Freddie had felt his excitement grow. Someone had once given him a book about whaling in the Pacific Ocean, and the drawing of Scammon's Lagoon running red with blood was one he looked at over and over.

He wondered if perhaps he should have been born a century earlier — have been the "gunner" who launched the harpoons that brought down the huge mammals. What a feeling of conquest that must have been to struggle with a fifty-foot-long prey and win! Freddie's palms grew damp just at the thought.

He wished he could conduct the new sport he had invented in broad daylight so that others could cheer him on. But they wouldn't. Other men weren't like him. That much he knew. So he had to hunt on moonlit nights such as this one. Even then, conditions had to be perfect for him to see the giant mammals — no cloud cover, bright moon, and close proximity to the whales.

Captain Hernandez was asleep in his cabin, and Freddie was sure that most of the crew were sleeping too. The Chief Mate sailed the ship at night, but he didn't take his job too seriously. Every morning when Freddie went to his navigator's post, he discovered that they were usually somewhat off course. So far nothing major had happened, and Freddie soon straightened them out.

Captain Hernandez was an easygoing guy. As long as the crew didn't do anything to endanger the safety of the ship, he tended to turn his back on minor transgressions. He had a vague idea that Freddie carried a high-powered rifle aboard. A few times at night, he thought he'd heard its muffled shot, and a couple of the other crew members had joked about their conquistador navigator.

The captain had never really seen the weapon though and as long as Freddie didn't carry it ashore, what was the harm in his shooting at the moon or whatever? The poor man was so near-sighted, he couldn't have hit the broad side of a barn — if there were barns at sea.

Freddie was a valuable crew member. Raised in America, he had shown up at the dock three years ago and asked Captain Hernandez for a job as a navigator. After an interview and his trial voyage with them, it was obvious that Freddie knew navigation. He mentioned having been in the U. S. Navy. The captain didn't ask how he had come to be a citizen of Colombia. Questions weren't his business. Delivering hardwoods to America was and getting paid for prompt delivery was even more important.

He told Freddie he would give him a chance. At the end of the first trip, he was put on permanently. The previous navigator had retired due to illness, and good help was hard to find.

On this night, after an hour of pacing the deck, Freddie gave up on seeing any whales even though his sixth sense told him they were there. He climbed down the ladder to make a quick check of his special cargo in the hold of the ship before returning to his bunk. There was more than a rifle that he was carrying.

Fifty kilo bundles of high-grade cocaine wrapped in waterproof sheeting camouflaged to look like seaweed. Before the rest of the crew boarded, he had hidden the drugs in a wooden crate behind one of the boilers and padlocked the box.

Each trip cost him $1000 in bribes to the crew members who knew the box was there. They were paid not to ask questions, and they didn't.

A thousand dollars was chicken feed compared to what Freddie got from the Cartel boss at the end of every successful delivery. He was paid $18,000 per kilo to transport the drugs — and that was less than the rate paid to pilots who ferried the stuff in planes equipped with high-tech electronic equipment including encoding and scrambling devices for secure communications and sensitive receivers that allowed them to eavesdrop on their pursuers.

Freddie wasn't complaining about the rate. On this trip, he had fifty kilos. That was $900,000. Sure he had to pay George, Les and Dirk $100,000 each for their role, but that still left $600,000 in his pocket. He already had a Swiss bank account in a phony name. And he hoped to make at least four or five delivery trips a year. Not bad for someone his commanding officer had once said "lacked leadership potential."

But even with the prospect of another payoff at the end of May, Freddie didn't feel especially cheerful. The woman he had been living with for the past two years had just kicked him out before this trip and said she never wanted to see him again. Ironically, her name was Maria.

"I sail on the *Si Maria*," he muttered to himself, "but I live with the *No Maria*."

She'd told him she was tired of his foul mouth and his unfaithful ways, but secretly Freddie suspected it was his looks. Saddled with heavy eyeglasses from childhood, he'd been the target of taunts all his life. The ultimate ridicule had come from a group of high school boys he'd grown up with in Nevada. Although his glasses corrected his vision enough for reading, he had never been able to have accurate depth perception at a distance.

In Sparks, outside Reno, where he'd been raised, all of his friends went hunting every spring and every fall. Freddie went with them. It was the thing to do and he hoped to make his peers respect him.

Freddie liked guns and as a teenager he often boasted about what kind of assault rifles he was going to buy when he had more money. He liked the idea of killing things. But he couldn't hit a quail or a chukker. He couldn't even hit a deer.

He gave up hunting with the guys, but he still practiced shooting every day. Sometimes he even missed the targets he nailed to trees, but when he did score a hit, the sound of splintering wood gave him satisfaction.

Aboard the lumber freighter, it had been quite by accident that he had discovered an easy target he could shoot from the *Si Maria* on his last trip. He wasn't sure why he'd taken his rifle along, but a week before they left, he decided to pack it in his trunk. Perhaps he could do a little shooting practice at night. A rifle such as his didn't ordinarily come with a silencer, but Freddie had a gunsmith make one. He wouldn't want to wake up anyone.

It was late November when they'd left Colombia — December when they reached Baja and then the U. S. coastline. One night around 2 a.m., when he was restless and couldn't sleep, he walked up on the deck just to sit and think. There was a full moon, and as he stood on the deck looking out over the illuminated water, the explosive snort of a gray whale spouting startled him.

They were within 20 yards of the huge creature. In the daylight hours, Captain Hernandez steered away from whales whenever he saw them. But now the captain was asleep and the Chief Mate was not as conscientious.

Instinctively, Freddie ran to get his gun. He felt a thrill as he loaded the Browning semiautomatic 30-06 rifle and put the specially-made silencer on it. When he returned to the deck, the whale was behind them. He saw its sleek gray head as he raised his rifle, aimed, and fired rapidly four times in a row.

He glanced anxiously over his shoulder to make sure no one from the wheelhouse was looking his way as he crouched behind an overhang. The bullets must have hit the water because there was no reaction from the whale.

He fired again — one, two, three, four, five shots. This time there was a huge spout of air from the whale and its giant body tipped almost vertically as it dove to the bottom. The thrash from its tail sent a huge swell that rocked the boat with the force of a sea squall.

On that night of his first hit, Freddie climbed back down the ladder and hid the gun under his bunk in his locker. For the first time in weeks, he slept really well. He didn't think about his troubles with women and he didn't think about his childhood or his parents, long since dead.

In the next two months, he managed to shoot at ten whales. There was only one occasion when he actually saw blood mixed in with the spume, but he had a feeling at least some of his hits had scored. Shooting things made him feel strong. Shooting whales made him feel invincible.

Now Freddie dismissed his scoreless night as unimportant. He got on his hands and knees and put the rifle and ammunition back in his locker. This was going to be a good trip from here on, he told himself firmly. At the end of it, he would be even richer than when he started. So what if he hadn't seen any whales tonight? There were many more nights to come and many more nights to kill.

They were just entering the phase of the full moon and clear weather was forecast all the way to the California-Oregon border. He climbed into his bunk, pulled up the thick wool blankets, and closed his eyes.

The Chief Mate opened his eyes from a light slumber as he saw the shadow of a man climbing down the ladder into the cabin area. Probably Freddie. Strange guy. Knew his job all right but rebuffed any attempts at conversation. Always kept to himself, and he'd heard from some of the crew members that he shot at things at night. Come to think of it, he was pretty sure he had heard a muffled rifle report once or twice. Oh well — to each his own.

The Chief Mate felt sleepy again. Not much to do during the night. Now he stood and made his way back to the wheelhouse. Was there a storm brewing?

Odd, he thought as he looked out over the calm sea. He couldn't even see whitecaps — just moonlight glancing off the dark water. Still, he was sure he sensed something in the air. He stood for a minute and then settled back down in his chair.

Chapter 5

Places to Go and People to See

Saturday, April 20th
Newport, Oregon

T he rain of the previous two days stopped early Saturday morning and gave way to a beautiful sunrise. Sunshine pouring in through the windows woke Kim at seven, and she got up, stretching contentedly at the thought of an unprogrammed weekend.

The night before when Julia and Megan had left to go home to Portland, Kim briefly considered visiting her parents in Salem. But the need to catch up on her studies and the appeal of time by herself won out.

As she dressed and ate breakfast, listening to a local radio station, Kim planned her day.

The three girls spent so little time in their apartment that it didn't really have a chance to get dirty, but Kim decided to sweep and mop the kitchen floor for good measure. Having all the water she wanted for cleaning was a luxury after her experience as a fire lookout in the Cascades the summer before. Never again would she take the basic necessities of life for granted.

By ten, the apartment was sparkling clean. Kim wandered down to the small library to pick up a book Dr. Bolny had recommended. She settled herself by the window and began to read the chapters on gray whale migration.

"You an orphan this weekend too?"

Kim jumped at the voice. Jack Reser, a graduate student she had met briefly, stood in the doorway.

"Yes, I guess I am," Kim said smiling. "And you?"

"Oh, my home's in Colorado. I don't go back except for Christmas. Last summer I worked here, and I expect to again this year. So how do you like the Marine Science Center so far?"

His friendly voice encouraged her to talk, and Kim soon found herself telling him about her indecision of a major and how she came to be a student at the coast this term. She left out the part about Marc.

"Aren't you the one who's a ham radio operator? I heard someone talking about your antenna-stringing activities."

Kim laughed.

"That must have been Dan. I had to crawl out on his window ledge to attach my dipole."

"Dipole?"

"Come on, I'll show you."

Jack followed Kim back to the apartment. She was glad she had cleaned it so well as he glanced appreciatively around the small quarters.

"The feminine touch," he said grinning at the small bouquet of daffodils she'd placed on the kitchen table. "About the only decoration we have in ours is Kurt's underwear. That guy never picks up anything."

Kim smiled.

"The ham rig's in here."

In a corner of her small bedroom, Kim's low-band transceiver sat on a wooden table. She turned it on and tuned it up on 20 meters. All she could hear was static, so she quickly flipped through the other frequency bands.

"At home, I have a three-element beam that rotates," she explained to Jack. "I can aim it in any direction in the world. This dipole is stationary, but this particular kind does allow me to use all frequency bands. However, right now, everything appears to be dead."

"Dead as in deceased?"

Jack raised his eyebrows quizzically.

"Well, maybe asleep would be a better term. Due to all sorts of factors like the bounce of radio signals, sun spots, position of the Earth, etc., certain times of day and year are better for getting through on different frequencies. When we don't hear anything at all, we call it dead. But that doesn't mean it won't come to life. I talked to Japan the first day of the term."

"What's that?"

Kim looked out the window, following Jack's pointing finger.

"Oh, that's my two-meter antenna. I stuck it on the side of the building. Here, I'll show you."

Kim detached the rubber antenna from her handheld and connected the small transceiver to the coax leading to the fixed antenna. She punched in the local repeater frequency. To her surprise, Gary from the Coast Guard Station was talking to another ham, N7WXA.

"N6GP from KA7SJP," she said after he signed.

"KA7SJP from N6GP. Well good morning, Kim. How are you?"

"Just fine, Gary, although I did have one minor adventure after I signed with you the other night. Say hello to a fellow student, Jack. We seem to be the only two students here for the weekend other than Tracie who's working in the gift shop today."

"Good morning, Jack. Are you a ham, too?"

"No, I'm not Gary, but this certainly looks fascinating. Kim has been telling me about the hobby."

"Say, you two, I'm just about at the Coast Guard Station now, so I'd better say good-bye. But if you have free time on your hands, stop by and I'll give you a tour of the place. I'll be on duty until eight tonight."

"Well?" Jack said after Kim said good-bye to Gary.

"Well what?"

"Do you have free time on your hands?"

She looked again at Jack. Blond, short, and stocky, he was the exact physical opposite of Marc. He smiled at her in open friendliness, and she found herself smiling back.

"I was going to work on a paper, but...I mean, yes, I do, I guess," Kim blushed as she stumbled over her words.

30

"How 'bout lunch then? I know this place that serves fantastic crab."

Kim laughed. Every place on the Oregon coast advertised fantastic crab.

"Do we have to catch it first?"

"Nope, just eat it."

"I'll meet you in the lobby in ten minutes — okay?"

"Okay."

Kim stood watching the empty doorway after he left. Mixed emotions flooded through her — emotions she thought she felt only for Marc.

"Oh don't be silly," she told herself aloud. "This isn't a date — and supposin' it is? I bet Marc is dating plenty."

She rushed into the bathroom to comb her hair.

Jack was waiting in the lobby. On the drive into town, they laughed and joked like old friends. After strolling around the waterfront in the spring sunshine for an hour or so, they headed over to the Coast Guard Station.

"Just a minute," Kim said as Jack prepared to open the car door. "N6GP from KA7SJP. Are you around, Gary?"

There was a long pause.

"Well, I guess he can't monitor all the time."

But just then a friendly voice came back.

"KA7SJP from N6GP. Hi Kim — I had a few minutes for a break and just stepped outside and turned this thing on. Where are you?"

"Right in front of the station," Kim said.

"Well, hang on — I'll be there."

Within seconds, a tall, distinguished-looking man in his mid-thirties came walking around the building. He was carrying a handheld transceiver much like Kim's.

"Hi, Kim," he said, extending his hand.

"Gary, this is Jack. Thanks for inviting us over. I've never been inside a Coast Guard Station before."

"Well, come on. I'll give you the grand tour."

They followed Gary as he showed them the immaculate quarters inside and the well-rigged boathouses down below. Kim shook her head in disbelief when he told them that some of their craft were able to sustain a 360 degree roll in the water.

"I bet you get called out on every kind of emergency imaginable," Jack said.

"Yes, we do," agreed Gary. "And that's what we're here for, but occasionally people waste our time. Want to see how we spent yesterday?"

They followed him into a boathouse and gasped. What appeared to be a seven-foot-tall man was hanging from a hook in the ceiling. Kim walked closer and saw that it was really a dummy. Burlap bags were tied together in a human shape and dressed in a navy blue polyester suit. The dummy even had gloves, boots and a hat.

"We got a call that there was a dead man floating in the kelp. Know what it cost to 'rescue' him? $2700 — that's taxpayer money, and it would have been more if weather conditions had allowed us to put up aircraft."

"Does that kind of thing happen often?" Kim asked.

"Fortunately, no. We're busy enough dealing with real emergencies."

"What about drug smuggling?" Jack questioned. "There was a big article in the paper last week about the increase of drugs in the Northwest. Some officials are speculating that they're coming in by sea."

"Drugs are an ongoing problem. Anytime we get a lead, we investigate," Gary said. "We don't routinely search ships, but we're certainly always on the lookout both in the air and at sea."

Kim and Jack stayed around for awhile and then thanked Gary.

"You bet — stop by anytime. And Kim, you might want to come to the local radio club meetings — we have an excellent group here. Want me to put your name on the list so you get the newsletter?"

"I'd like that Gary — thank you."

Kim and Jack drove back to the Marine Science Center. It had been good to take a break; however, they both had studying to do. They said good-bye and Kim went back to her apartment to get busy. She settled down by the living room, but it was difficult to concentrate.

Somehow, being with Jack, made memories of Marc even more painful. She wondered if anyone could ever fill the void he'd left in her life.

Well, if you feel that way, why didn't you just say yes to his proposal? she lectured herself. *Because I'm not ready to make that commitment yet*, she answered. *If he doesn't understand that, he doesn't understand me.*

The mental conversation was small solace for the way she felt. Kim sighed and turned back to her texts.

Chapter 6

Deadly Seas

Saturday, April 20th, 10 p.m.
Just north of Newport

"**C**an't you make this thing go any faster?" Dirk
shouted to George who sat at the back of the Zodiac,
manning the engine.

His words were lost in the wind. What had been a sunny
day had changed abruptly at nightfall to gusty, gale
conditions. Another spring storm was coming in. The three
men in wetsuits bent over, protecting themselves from the
waves that sloshed over the edges of the boat. They had put
the boat in the water as close as they could to the secluded
rocky cave north of Newport, but in this weather, every foot
seemed like a mile.

After slamming against several rocks in the surf line, they
reached their goal at last. Les tossed a rope around a rock at
the opening to the cave and held the small craft as steady as
he could while George and Dirk slid overboard.

With underwater flashlights and snorkels, they made
their way into the deep cave. The surf action was less in here,
but the noise of the waves lapping inside the cave was eerie.

Dirk stayed close to George.

On a rock ledge just above the water line, their remaining
four bundles of cocaine were anchored securely to pylons. Dirk
untied the ropes holding the waterproof packages and handed
two to George. Carefully, they half swam, half walked back to
the opening of the cave. Les placed the drugs under his seat
and then helped the men in.

The wind was blowing to the north so the Zodiac moved
back along the coast precariously fast. Dirk kept them out
beyond the surf line to stay away from the rocks. When they

were opposite the small beach where they'd entered the water, it was all they could do to maneuver the boat through the rough surf without capsizing. As soon as they reached chest-deep water, they jumped out and pulled the boat ashore.

For a few minutes, they lay breathing heavily on the beach before climbing the rocky trail that led back to the road. George slung all four bundles of cocaine over his shoulders while Les and Dirk carried the boat between them.

Their truck was parked in the shelter of some trees, and the men moved quickly, stowing their gear. Whenever a car passed, they crouched down behind the truck until the headlights were long gone.

George peeled off his wetsuit jacket and jumped into the driver's side.

"Come on — hurry it up!" he yelled to the other two.

The windows of the cab fogged up completely from the moisture on their wetsuits and their exhausted breathing. George cursed as he leaned forward to wipe the windshield with the palm of his hand. He continued on down the road for a mile and then made a sharp right hand turn onto a deserted road. When he was satisfied, they were well away from the highway, he stopped the truck.

His own urgency transferred to the other men and they hurriedly peeled out of their wetsuits and scrambled into the jeans and flannel shirts they had in the back of the truck.

George stuffed the wetsuits into a crate in the back of the truck and shoved the drug bundles under an old canopy beside the air pump they used for the boat. The Zodiac was deflated until it could be folded over to fit in through the canopy.

"I wish we could leave that thing out in the woods," Les complained.

"Too risky — you never know where nosey hikers are going to turn up. A boat in the woods is definitely a question. One in the back of our pickup is easily explained. We like to crab in the bay."

"Where are our crabbing rings then, Boss?" Dirk snorted.

"Good point. Maybe we'll buy a couple on our way in next time, except I don't see how anything else is going to fit back there. Maybe we'll strap them on top. But now, gentlemen, it's time to head for Spokane. We can be there before sunup and make this drop. That means in less than two weeks when Fred comes with the next drop, we get paid.

"After a little shut-eye, this time tomorrow, we'll be ready to party. Any takers? Or have you guys spent all your money from the last payoff?"

"Not me, boss," said Dirk. "I still got five hundred bucks left."

George laughed. When word got back to the Cartel boss that all deliveries had been made successfully, Freddie was given the okay to pay them. Usually, he was able to do it in Newport, but if need be the men were only too willing to drive to another port to meet him.

George was salting his money away, waiting for the day he could be out of this business for good. Les and Dirk were spending their share almost as fast as they got it. Each had already bought a fancy sports car. It didn't go with their image as seasonal fishermen to have the cars at the coast so George had insisted they put them in storage in Portland.

"Let's go," said Les, shoving Dirk into the middle of the truck seat. "I want a sixteen-ounce Porterhouse steak for breakfast."

The men settled into the truck and began the eight hour drive to Spokane. They were looking forward to a little time off. This last shipment had been spread out to six different cities. They had worked hard for their money, and they had yet to receive it. Occasionally Dirk and Les questioned the way they were paid, but George told them to be patient. No pay for drugs until the job was completed.

There was always the chance Freddie would cheat them, but he didn't think so — he needed them to do his dirty work as much as they needed the money.

Someone named Curly was to meet them at a motel room in Spokane. If the boss men were happy, then the whole delivery scheme would begin again.

George was the only one of the three who knew any of the itinerary of the drops. He had once served a brief prison term with Fred Walner. Both were in for selling drugs. During their probation, Freddie had split for South America.

"But I'll be in touch," he'd told George.

Two years went by before he heard through a mutual friend that Freddie would be in a certain bar in San Pedro for two hours on a Friday night. "Be there," the message said.

When George had arrived on that fateful Friday night last fall, Freddie was sitting with two other men from the *Si Maria*. He excused himself and went to a private table with George.

"Hey, Fred, good to see you," George said, clapping him on the shoulder.

"Freddie; it's Freddie Vasquez," Freddie answered. "See," he said, pulling his passport from a pocket and flipping it open briefly.

George smiled, waiting for an explanation. The cellmate he remembered was pale and clean shaven with short black hair. Now he wore his hair collar length and was darkly tanned. He wondered why he'd changed his last name to a Spanish one. Freddie ignored his questioning look and began a very cursory explanation of the operation.

"We have some goods that need delivery to the Northwest and we're looking for a new courier. Interested?"

George was.

Now he reflected on his good fortune at having shared a cell with Freddie. Freddie had the connections to make them big money. The demand for cocaine was rising every day in the United States. More and more consumers were paying incredible prices, risking their lives, and courting jail sentences to inhale or smoke the white powder that made them feel good for a short while. Even George had to admit it was crazy, but there was lots of money to be made. Drug addicts were an easy target and George had always been a good shot.

* * *

Saturday, April 20th, 11:30 p.m.

Just south of Santa Barbara, Silver Star and his mother made their way steadily toward their northern destination. Driven by hunger and instinct, the nursing mother pushed her body through the water. In olden days, whalers called the returning animals "dry skins" because their blubber was seriously depleted after their long journey.

Survival depended on returning to the rich Arctic seas. Moon, even more physically drained than the young mother, lagged far behind. She would migrate until she died. It was as simple as that. The mighty heart within her aging body pulsed rhythmically as she forced herself on. It was almost midnight. They would keep swimming all night, except for occasional short rests on the surface. Moon's pace slowed. It was impossible to keep up with the younger, more vigorous animals. By the time Silver Star and his mother were opposite Goleta Beach in Santa Barbara, Moon was a full mile behind.

* * *

At midnight, the lights of Santa Barbara twinkled in the distance. Freddie Vasquez crept from his bed. By the sound of the engines, he could tell that the Chief Mate had throttled down slightly. That was a sign that he wasn't paying close attention to his duties. In fact, if the mate was sure the captain was asleep, he might not even be in the wheelhouse at all. He and a couple of the other crew members liked to play cards.

Freddie pulled the seaman's chest out from under his bunk and opened it. His rifle lay under some clothing. Quickly, he loaded it and put the silencer on the barrel. No one was up at this hour as he climbed the ladder to the back deck. Again, a beautiful moonlit night — the kind of night meant for conquests. He lay on his stomach near the railing, making sure that he was not in direct view of the wheelhouse.

Part of the excitement was waiting for his prey. He spread his feet slightly, gripping the deck with the toes of his rubber-soled shoes, and cradled the rifle in his arms. An hour went by before he saw anything. Then the water started to look rough one hundred yards to the port side. Freddie felt his heart pound as the surface broke and the scarred head of a gray whale broke the surface.

Instinctively, he fired — once, twice, three times. There was one giant thrashing motion from the whale's tail, and then it disappeared. Freddie waited, hoping it might offer itself as a target again.

* * *

Even a mile away, the percussion of the shot traveled through the water and resonated within the sonar cavities of Silver Star and his mother. Unlike their hunted ancestors, they had never heard a gunshot. Instinctively, fear quickened the pace of the young whale's mother. Urging her body forward, she increased her speed to the limit she thought her baby could endure. They must get away from that terrible noise.

For Moon, one mile behind, there was no escape. One of the three bullets had hit home, driving deep into her brain. Unlike most of the shots Freddie fired at whales, this one had hit a vital place. Disoriented and unable to maintain surface breathing, she sank toward the ocean floor.

For several terrible minutes, the huge animal thrashed, trying to stabilize her position in the water. She needed air, but she couldn't bring her body to the surface. Desperately she tried to right herself as her bulk rolled far to the right side, almost turning her upside down. As her oxygen supply ran out, she continued to struggle valiantly. Gradually, the memories of decades dimmed and closed as the giant mammal convulsed again and again and then finally lay still, drifting downward in the warm Pacific current.

Chapter 7

Escargots and French Fries

Sunday, April 21st
Spokane

W hile Les and Dirk snored away in the truck cab, George drove through the night. Across the Willamette Valley to Interstate 5. North to the edge of Portland, east through the windy Columbia Gorge, northeast to Kennewick, Pasco, and on to Spokane. The sun was just coming up as the trio rolled into the eastern Washington city. George drove to the Acorn Motor Inn on the outskirts of town.

The drug drop was made smoothly. As in the weeks before, they didn't know the contact person — just had a name and a room number. When George arrived and knocked three times, "Curly" quickly opened the door to room 212. Les and Dirk were still asleep in the truck.

Curly unzipped the duffel bag George was carrying and briefly examined the contents. He transferred the bundles into a large green bag and handed the empty duffel back to George.

"Looks okay — had better be. You'll get a call in a couple of weeks in Newport. Be there."

The two parted without so much as a handshake.

Les and Dirk were startled awake as George opened the truck door.

"I'm hungry," Dirk declared as George drove back out of the parking lot.

"Shut up," said George. "You're always hungry."

Not another word was spoken until the three of them arrived at a motel on the other end of town. This time, George and Dirk waited in the truck while Les got them a room.

"I told her we'd been driving all night and planned on sleeping. No problem, she says — just hang out the Do Not Disturb sign."

Sleeping was exactly what George had in mind, but Dirk and Les were well-rested. As George stripped down to his underwear and climbed into bed. Dirk and Les spread the contents of their wallets on the other bed, seeing just how much money they had left to blow. Their motel room in Newport was paid through the end of the month, and if need be, they could live on beans and rice. The prospect of more money coming soon made them almost giddy.

After stern warnings from George about not drawing attention to themselves, Les and Dirk left the motel, with George reluctantly allowing them to take the truck. Whenever there were drugs on board, George did all the driving. But now that it was empty, he decided it was okay for the two to go out to breakfast and perhaps buy themselves some new clothes.

"Just don't do anything that will make people remember you."

"Right, Boss."

Like kids out of school, the two drove into town.

"Ham n' Eggs — $3.99" proclaimed the sign in front of the all-night diner.

"Here we go. Steak sounds good to me. Medium rare," Dirk said.

They parked the truck and entered the cheerful red and white cafe decorated with American flags. Locals sat at the counter, drinking coffee, reading the paper, and sharing gossip. Dirk and Les took a corner booth in the back, far away from a family with three preschool children who were giggling as they blew the paper covers off their straws at each other.

"What kind of a place is this anyway?" Dirk growled. "The largest steak on the menu is eight ounces."

The waitress, a gray-haired plump woman who looked like she had served plenty of orders of ham and eggs in her life, rolled her eyes.

"What size did you want, sir?"

She said the "sir" under her breath as though she hated addressing Dirk with that title. Both men were unshaven and smelled like they needed a bath.

"A pound at least."

"What if we give you two steaks, sir?"

Dirk looked up at her and smiled, exposing stained crooked teeth.

"Why that would be real nice, sweetie. And make sure they're medium rare with a couple of eggs over easy and lots of hash browns."

"And you, sir?"

"Aw, just gimme a large order of biscuits and gravy and some Tabasco sauce," Les answered.

The waitress hurried to the back. Frankly, she wondered whether the pair had any money. They didn't look especially prosperous. But to her surprise, when it came time for them to leave, Dirk plopped a five-dollar bill down on the table as a tip.

They paid at the front counter and burped noisily on the way out the door. The waitress sighed with relief as they left, slipped the tip in her pocket, and returned to the other customers. Odd, how you just never could tell about people, she mused.

"Well, where to now?" Les asked, a toothpick hanging out of his mouth.

"Let's see — it's 11 o'clock. Stores are open. How about getting some new duds? That way, we won't have to wash these," he laughed. "Just throw them away."

They drove down a main street toward the center of town.

"Hey, I thought we were going to a mall," Les said as Dirk pulled into the parking lot of A. G. Western Specialties.

"Always wanted some fancy cowboy stuff — one of these days, I'm gonna buy me a ranch in Montana."

Dirk snorted, but he followed Les into the store willingly. The young clerk at the counter looked slightly apprehensive as he saw the two unkempt men pawing through hundred-dollar designer-brand western shirts.

"May I help you?" he asked starting to get up.

"Nope, not yet — just keep your seat, Steve," said Dirk, reading the young man's name tag.

"Hey, look at this!"

Dirk turned to Les who was holding up a bright maroon shirt and turquoise jeans.

"Definitely you," Dirk laughed.

Nervously, Steve busied himself checking invoices at the counter. He was beginning to wish he weren't on duty alone. These guys gave him the creeps. He watched as the pair made their way down each aisle, trying on ten-gallon hats, snake-skin boots, and silver-studded cowhide belts. The two of them disappeared into dressing rooms carrying huge piles of clothing, and soon their hoots of laughter came from the back of the store.

Steve tried to ignore the noise as he busied himself with a lady customer looking for a birthday present for her husband.

"Sounds like someone's having fun," she commented as their laughter rose in volume.

Suddenly, the dressing room doors burst open and Dirk came out first, outfitted in a plaid purple shirt, purple jeans with rhinestones on the back pockets, gray rattlesnake-skin boots, and a white suede hat with a purple band. Les followed, all in green. Green stone-washed jeans, light-green silk shirt, forest-green leather vest, green hat, and dark-green leather boots. A green and white kerchief added the finishing touch.

"Well whadya think?" Dirk asked the clerk.

"Uh, uh, oh very nice gentlemen. Did you want those things?"

"Yup, and we want to wear them. Here are all the price tags."

Dirk slapped a fist full of tags on the counter. Steve began entering them into the register.

There's no way — just no way they're going to pay for all this, he thought as he added up the total.

"Eight hundred and ninety-two dollars and thirty-nine cents," he said to Les.

"No problem," Les laughed, turning to Dirk who handed him four hundred dollars. He laid that along with five more hundred dollar bills of his own on the counter.

Steve gasped and quickly made change.

"Would you like me to wrap up your old clothes?"

"Nope, keep them or give them to charity or something," Dirk said.

The two exited the store, slapping each other on the back and saying "Howdy Partner." Steve waited until he was sure they were gone and then went into the dressing room. All of their clothes including their underwear lay on the floor in a heap.

"Gross," he said.

He grabbed a paper bag and gingerly kicked the clothes into it with his foot.

"Think we ought to go back to the motel?"

"Are you kidding, Les? George will sleep all day. What would we do there — watch TV and listen to him snore? Let's catch a movie and then go to a high-class restaurant and then maybe find a bar or two — maybe a girl for each of us. What do you think?"

"Right on, Partner."

The two burst out laughing again at their own cleverness. They were still chortling as they stood in line for "Bloodsuckers," the latest Grade B movie. When it was over, they slipped into the theater next to it and watched the last half of "Visitors from Alpha."

"Five o'clock," said Dirk, blinking in the lobby lights.

"Man, we skipped lunch, and my stomach's telling me about it."

"How about another steak?"

"No, this time we're going to live high class — I saw a place called Chez Pierre as we drove in — bet that's either French or Italian. You ever had French food, Les?"

"Tacos and spaghetti and Chinese food — guess that's all from other countries."

"Come on — let's go get some culture."

Dirk curved his little finger in the air and pretended to be drinking out of a teacup.

The maitre d' of the Chez Pierre was as thrilled to see the two garishly dressed cowboys as the clerk of A. G.'s Western Speciatlies had been. He seated them in a back corner behind a potted fig tree, hoping that their presence wouldn't destroy the sophisticated atmosphere his staff worked so hard to maintain.

"Bon jour."

"Huh?" Dirk responded.

"Good evening, gentlemen. May I get you a cocktail or perhaps a bottle of wine from our cellar?"

"Yeah, wine. Red stuff, and if it's any good, you ought to bring it up in the kitchen."

Les laughed at his own wit. The waiter focused on some distant object and waited patiently.

"And perhaps an appetizer before your meal."

"We got plenty of appetite, but bring it on anyway. Whatever you think tastes good and is gut-filling too."

"I would recommend the coq au vin for an entree and les escargots in garlic sauce to start."

"S cars? That like a Ford? We just want something to eat. But bring them things on anyway, whatever they are. And the more garlic, the better."

"Very well, sir."

The waiter returned promptly with a bottle of red wine. He dispensed with the ceremony of offering it to taste to one of them and just filled their glasses. Les guzzled his down immediately and burped. The waiter fled to the kitchen.

By the time he came back with their appetizer, the bottle was drained and under the table.

"That's pretty good stuff," Dirk said. "Lay another one on us."

"As you wish, gentlemen. Here are les escargots in garlic sauce."

He lifted the lids from two small platters and placed the steaming dishes in front of the men. Les looked down at the small creatures in front of him. He poked at one gingerly with his fork. He turned it over and put his face practically down to eye level with the plate to study its contents. A red flush of anger crept up his neck as he jumped to his feet.

"Snails!" he shouted in a voice that drew stares from all over the restaurant. "Snails! Here we come in here respectable and all and you treat us like dirt — trying to feed us snails. Why I oughta..."

Dirk caught his fist before it connected with the waiter's face. In minutes, two men in business suits were beside Les and Dirk. Each man gripped one of the cowboys and within seconds the pair found themselves in the street. The manager followed them out.

"You owe us money for the wine, but I'll forgive your bill if you'll just leave now."

"Just because we ain't ritzy, you didn't have to serve us snails."

Les's voice was more of a whine. Dirk took him by the arm and led him to the truck.

"Come on — let's get out of here."

"I'm hungry," Les complained. "Hungry and mad."

Dirk drove back toward the motel on the main street of town.

"Rancho Burgers — how about a burger and fries, Les?"

"And onion rings and a chocolate shake — better than any old snails. In fact, I think I'll have a double burger."

Chapter 8

Whales!

Sunday, April 21st, noon
Newport, Oregon

After several hours of note -aking, Kim decided to take a lunch break. She wandered down the halls of the Marine Science Center toward the lobby and bumped into Florence Bund, the woman in charge of volunteers who manned the whale-watch sites.

"You look worried; what's the matter?" Kim asked.

"Oh, Dr. Bolny requested that we do a special whale count this weekend for a project of his. I had arranged volunteers but I just got a call that our husband and wife team scheduled to work up at Rocky Creek can't come in — their son is ill. Guess I'll go substitute. We had wanted to start the counts exactly at noon."

"Wait, I'll go. I know you have lots to do here. I did two days of whale watching over spring break and I loved it. Just tell me what he wants. I'll enjoy the excuse to be outside," Kim said.

"Oh, you're a dear. I'll get the papers for you. Basically, it's the same data we collect during the winter and spring vacations. He wants to gather some statistics to compare with figures he took last year."

"Is this because of the dead grays?"

"Yes, I think so."

Kim went to her room to get a warm coat and hat and her binoculars. She picked up her two-meter radio and ran back to the lobby to wait for Florence. She was grateful she didn't run into Jack in the halls. She had a hunch he'd volunteer to come along.

And what would be wrong with that? she asked herself. Since when haven't you liked male companionship? She had no answer for herself, but she knew she didn't feel like company.

Florence returned with the needed papers and Kim took them to her car along with an apple and some pretzels. The weatherman had predicted rain, but as if laughing at man's predictions, the sun had come out. Kim admired the beautiful rugged coastline as she drove north to Rocky Creek State Park.

Almost every turnout on Highway 101 was filled with cars and RVs. Some people were flying kites, others were watching for whales, and others were simply walking along the bluffs, enjoying the day.

She arrived at the park and pulled her car into a space at the edge of the lot and grabbed her binoculars. At a picnic bench right out on the bluff, a gray-haired couple with an energetic Airedale sat eating their lunch. They smiled at her as she approached.

"Hi," Kim said. "Have you seen any whales today?"

"As a matter of fact, we have — a couple went by about fifteen minutes ago."

"How far out were they?"

"About halfway to the horizon. We didn't bring binoculars, but it looked like two — one spout was definitely bigger than the other."

"Most likely a mother and a baby. They're heading back to the Arctic to feed for the summer."

"What a long journey," the woman said. "And to think I'm tired just from walking Jocko here."

At the mention of his name, the dog stood and began pulling eagerly on the leash. The couple laughed at their pet's antics and got up.

"Guess it's time to go, dear," the man said to his wife. "Let's put the lunch stuff back in the van and then walk Jocko just a little more before we drive down the coast to Gold Beach."

After inviting them to stop by the Marine Science Center for some whale lectures, Kim told the couple good-bye and walked to the edge of the bluff. The wind had calmed down, smoothing the whitecaps on the sea. A perfect whale-watching day. She scanned the horizon in much the same way that she'd scanned the forests as a lookout. Left to right in a repetitive pattern. The whales were there — it was just a question of looking in the right place as they surfaced and blew.

A half hour went by before she saw her first pair — a mother and a baby. Like the man had said, they were about halfway to the horizon. Kim noted their position in her notes. Ten minutes later, four more went by. Maybe three adults and one baby, but she couldn't be sure. One of them breached, jumping high in the air and splashing impressively as it crashed into the ocean. Kim felt a thrill at watching the magnificent creatures, even from a distance.

Gary had mentioned that several local hams often volunteered as whale watchers. She wondered if any of them were part of Dr. Bolny's special project today. She turned on her small two-meter rig, called CQ, and then held it to her ear to listen.

A woman named Linda at Yaquina Head came back to her.

"KA7SJP this is KD6JPS — sounds like we've got the same call letters — just a little mixed up."

Kim laughed and visited with her. It was always fun to meet new people on the air. Linda lived in California but enjoyed watching the whales so much that she and her husband made an annual spring trip just to help with the counts. She sounded all excited as she reported that a group of eight whales had just passed.

"You should see us down here — we're still jumping up and down. What a sight that was!"

Kim looked at her watch — she was at least ten miles from Linda — that would mean four hours until the whales reached her. Well, it was one now. She just might stick around.

She had barely signed with Linda when another ham called her.

"KA7SJP from N7DRP."

This·time it was a woman visiting the coast in her motor home.

"Heard you two talking about whales and wondered what that was all about."

"Oh, we're involved in a special project for the Marine Science Center. If you'd like to stop by, I'll give you some more information."

"Sounds interesting, Kim, but I'm on my way to a family reunion so I had better keep going. Good luck to you though. Hope you spot a lot of them."

Kim thanked her and signed. She was about to turn off her rig to save the batteries when an unexpected voice caught her by surprise.

"KA7SJP from KA7ITR."

Kim jumped. Marc! For a minute she was too stunned to reply.

"KA7ITR from KA7SJP. Where are you?"

"Just leaving the Marine Science Center. I didn't have anything to do this afternoon and thought I'd surprise you. A lady named Florence told me where you are. I'll be right there —if that's okay," he added as an afterthought.

"Well, sure it's okay."

"Good, I want to talk to you."

His voice sounded unusually serious.

"About...?" Kim questioned.

"Just want to talk to you."

"I'll be waiting. KA7ITR from KA7SJP clear."

"KA7ITR clear."

Kim turned off her radio and sat down on the bench. Emotion flowed through her as she ran her fingers through her hair in an effort to straighten her wind-blown curls. What if Jack had been spending the afternoon with her?

Well, what if he had been? she asked herself. Did she think they'd be jealous of each other? After all, Jack was a fellow student. Period. Still it would have been nice of Marc to let her know he was coming. Guess he still takes me for granted, she thought with just a twinge of resentment. But all that vanished at the sight of his familiar truck.

She ran to greet him.

* * *

Sunday, April 21st, 3 p.m.
Morro Bay, California

Aboard the *Si Maria*, Freddie Vasquez nodded in the warm sunshine pouring through the cabin window. His navigation charts were spread out before him. They had just docked to unload a small shipment of hardwoods for this California coastal town. Several children stood on the dock, hoping that the huge crane, now sitting idle, would swing the logs ashore. The original itinerary showed that they would be here a few hours. Apparently, that had changed. He turned to ask the First Mate.

"Didn't you hear? There's a shortage of personnel on the dock to unload. We might be here a day or two. Almost everyone else has gone ashore."

Freddie leaned back in his chair and closed his eyes. Although he had slept soundly after his nighttime hunt, it had still been a short night. He would just doze for a few minutes here and then wander into town.

He awoke with a start. The bad dream had come back. The one with ghostly voices he could never place. The voices seemed to beckon to him, to invite him to join them. He wished he could see the creatures behind the soft whispers — perhaps if he could, they wouldn't seem so evil. But to see them meant to go deeper into sleep with them. To ask them who they were. With a shudder, Freddie drew back into wakefulness.

His ex-wife in Colombia used to hate the dreams as much as Freddie did.

"My poor Freddie," she said as he awoke drenched in sweat one night the first week they were married. "What is the matter?"

Freddie never told her. It was too long a story. The dreams had started back in Hawaii at the end of six years in the Navy. He was a licensed Second Mate and a competent navigator's assistant. Then things started going terribly wrong. His first wife left him. He began having dark fits of depression.

He was pretty much a loner, but on a lonely night in Honolulu, Freddie accepted an invitation to a party. That was where he used crack cocaine for the first time. He was no stranger to marijuana — this was his first experience with hard stuff. For thirty minutes, Freddie felt a high such as he had never known. Then the hallucinations began. That night when he returned to the base, he became so sick in the early morning hours that he was put in the hospital. It didn't take the Navy doctors long to figure out what he had taken.

A few days later when he returned to duty, he was severely reprimanded and warned that any further transgressions could result in his expulsion from the service. For two months, Freddie heeded the warning. But when loneliness and depression took over, he was drawn to the men he'd met off the base. Before long, he was hooked, his body demanding the white powder.

"From your records, I see that you were considered a fine navigator. Right now, you're a disgrace."

Those were the words of his commanding officer as he was discharged from the Navy. They set up appointments for him in a drug rehabilitation clinic. Freddie never went. He stayed on in Hawaii as he had no desire to go back to the states. There was no one there who cared about him and certainly no one he cared about. He'd made some connections in Hawaii — connections that promised a living.

Those didn't work out either. On a trip to L.A. to deliver "goods," and high on drugs himself, he was arrested. He received a two-year jail sentence. That was when he met George and that was when he vowed he'd never be arrested again. The only good thing about prison was that he was forced to give up his drug habit. When he got out, he set out to make a new life for himself.

He worked for awhile around the shipyards but soon became bored with the menial labor. A visiting crewman on a South American freighter told him there were opportunities in Colombia. He even gave him the name of a couple of freighter captains who were hiring.

One of them hinted pretty broadly that there was plenty of money to be made in other trades as well. Freddie didn't ask what he meant — he knew: drugs. Vowing to himself that this time he would be involved in the dealing end of the business rather than the using, he made the decision to go.

Freddie used his paychecks to buy a one-way ticket to Bogota and to get a phony passport — one that couldn't be checked against his parole record. He knew a little Spanish and felt confident he could pick up the language quickly. Back in his high school days, he had been a fairly decent student. Learning things he wanted to do had always been easy.

His first few months in Bogota were fairly traumatic. It was harder to find work than he'd been told. It took a lot of looking to hook up with the right people — the people he felt could make him rich.

He kept his promise to himself not to use cocaine for exactly three months. But then he decided occasional use wouldn't hurt. Actually, it seemed to him that his thoughts were clearer when he was using. He was sure nobody could tell. Once he got the job on the *Si Maria*, he tried to kick the habit but found he couldn't. So he rationalized that if he just used the stuff every few days, no one would be the wiser. He told himself he wasn't an addict. He just liked to feel better every once in a while.

In the daytime he believed himself. At night when ghosts reached out to him, he wondered just what lay ahead. All of this went through his mind as he looked out at the small tourist town of Morro Bay. He shook his head, stood up, stretched, and filled his coffee cup. It looked like there was zero activity on the dock — he might as well take a walk and look around.

Chapter 9

Another Death at Sea

Monday, April 22nd
Santa Barbara, California

On Monday following Marc's visit, Kim found herself so distracted that she could barely concentrate. Sunday afternoon had not gone well at all. At first when Marc arrived, it seemed like old times. She was just happy to see him, but then they got into an argument about something silly. Kim couldn't even remember what it was.

"You're just so stubborn," she accused Marc.

He laughed bitterly.

"And I suppose you're not?"

That hurt. Kim turned her back to him and walked to the bluff to scan for whales. To her surprise, she heard his truck engine starting. She turned around to see him leaving the parking lot without so much as a wave. Instinctively, she grabbed her two-meter rig but then slowly reattached it to her belt.

"If that's the way he's going to be, well just let him!" she said to the waves.

Tears rolled down her cheeks as she declared her indpendence, and an hour later when the group of whales did arrive, she didn't feel much joy.

Monday, she tried to busy herself but the hollow ache inside kept pulling at her. She tried her best not to think of the Marc she'd rescued from the snow on Mt. Jefferson nearly two years ago — of the shy, young man who had been her best friend ever since. They'd had so many thrilling adventures together and had become so close that Kim used to joke that the code key she used was a "telepathic key" instead of a telegraphic one. Was all that gone? Couldn't they even be friends?

"Boy, you look like you lost your best friend," Jack said at a break.

"I think I did," Kim said softly.

"Want to talk about it?"

"I don't think so, but thanks."

She reached out and touched Jack on the arm lightly and smiled.

"Well, anytime you want to, I'm here. Don't even need an appointment."

They walked down the hall together and then split up as Jack went to work in the weather-tracking room, and Kim continued on to the bone lab. It was her favorite place to work. Despite the smell of dead animals they were dissecting, she was fascinated by the process of putting together skeletons and identifying them.

Someone had actually found the skull of a gray whale, and the huge bony structure took up one whole corner of the room. With the help of a car jack, Megan and Kim had propped the mouth open to better show off the baleen attached to the upper jaw. The fringed baleen formed an effective mesh that trapped the whale's food.

"Wonder how you died?" Kim said, patting the skull they had named 'Bertha.' "Do we know how old this one is?"

"About ten, Dr. Bolny thinks — so it didn't die of old age," Megan said.

The girls busied themselves cataloguing bones, and Kim finally lost herself in her work. It wasn't until nighttime that her sorrow over what had happened with Marc resurfaced. She spent most of the night tossing and turning. It seemed like she'd only been asleep a few minutes when Julia woke her.

"What time is it?" Kim asked sleepily.

"Just seven, but Dr. Bolny has called a special meeting of all the marine science students. We're supposed to be in the auditorium by 7:30."

Kim flew out of bed, dressed, and ran downstairs. The students were speculating on reasons for the meeting as they filed into the auditorium. Dr. Bolny was on stage and came right to the point.

"I know I have some seminars scheduled today and tomorrow, and that a few of you were going out on the research vessel with me this afternoon. But there's been a development. Another dead gray whale has washed up near Santa Barbara. This one appears to have died within the last 24 hours so we may be able to tell something. I've been asked to come down and examine it before it's buried."

There was a hush in the audience as Dr. Bolny continued.

"I wish I could take one or two of you with me, but the grant money just isn't there. If any of you has an airplane ticket in your pocket, I'd welcome the company."

There was appreciative laughter from the students — most of whom were having financial problems enough just staying in school. Kim didn't laugh. Her Uncle Steve, the ham radio operator who had originally gotten her interested in the hobby, flew all over the world solving electromagnetic interference problems. As a result, he had tons of frequent flyer miles. This year for Christmas, he'd given Kim, her brother, and her parents each a ticket good anywhere on the West Coast.

She knew Brandon and her parents were going to Disneyland in June. Kim hadn't decided what to do with hers. But would it seem presumptuous to ask to go with Dr. Bolny? There were graduate students who were a lot more qualified than she was. After the group broke, she told Julia and Megan of her dilemma.

"Go tell him," urged Julia. "Actually most of the graduate students are so busy on projects, they wouldn't want to take two days out — and there's no one here who's actually studying gray whales. Mindy's area is sea lions; Jack's is salmon." She ticked off the students and their research papers.

Shyly, Kim walked to the door of Dr. Bolny's office. He was scurrying around, throwing things in a briefcase while giving instructions to his secretary, Liz.

"Call Dr. Hopkins and tell him I'll have to take a raincheck on that dinner; mail this packet to Professor Mendez in Mexico City; take..."

He stopped mid-sentence when he realized Kim was standing in the doorway.

"Were you joking about the free ticket?"

"What? Oh! Free airplane ticket. I was joking. Why? Do you have one?"

Quickly, she explained, afraid Dr. Bolny might laugh, but he didn't.

"Go pack your bag. This is a great opportunity for you. If you've got a camera, take it. We have to be in Portland by noon, so run. Should be back tomorrow night."

Kim hesitated a minute, making sure he was serious. Obviously he was, because he turned his back and continued giving instructions to his secretary. Kim flew to her room and threw some clothes in a sports bag. She talked nonstop while she ran around grabbing things.

"Can you believe it? I'm actually going. Wonder if Dr. Bolny will be able to tell what killed it? Wouldn't it be great if he could solve the mystery and save the whales?"

Julia and Megan watched her smiling.

"And to think you were shy of asking to go."

"Right. Well thanks for making me do it. You two are the greatest."

Sticking her two-meter rig in her purse, she waved good-bye and dashed down the hall. Dr. Bolny was in the lobby. They half-trotted to the parking lot and climbed into his car. It was a three hour drive to the airport and it was 9 o'clock already.

* * *

Les and Dirk didn't do a very good job of heeding George's warning not to draw attention to themselves. On Monday, they got kicked out of a bar for fighting with one of the customers. They moved on to another bar and were asked to leave after they made rowdy advances toward a woman sitting alone. Les wagered his last hundred dollars on a pool game, and when he lost, punched the guy in the nose. The pool hall owner escorted him to the door with the warning that if he ever came back, he would call the police.

"Trouble with the people in this town is that they don't know how to have fun," Dirk complained to Les as the two of them reluctantly made their way back to the motel in the wee hours of Tuesday after having run out of money.

George was awake and waiting for them and he was furious.

"You left at eight and said you were just going to a movie. Where have you been?"

"Just seeing the sights, George old boy. Relax."

George sighed and went back to bed. He would dump these two, but for the most part they were reliable. And they knew the Oregon coastline like the backs of their hands. He didn't really think he could do the pickups all by himself. Still, if they didn't keep a lower profile, they'd wind up in jail on drunk and disorderly charges. The last thing George wanted was for someone to start investigating their past.

None of them had a clean record.

"We could have a pickup as early as the 25th," George told them when they finally woke up Tuesday morning. "Let's go back tonight and get settled."

"Did you tell them we wanted the room back?"

"Yeah, remember, I paid for the whole month. I told the lady we were going on a fishing trip for a few days. No problem — that place is such a dump, I doubt she has people standing in line."

"And we'll get our next payments the 25th too? Right?" Les questioned.

"Yeah, sure. That's the way it works unless for some reason Freddie can't meet with me — then I'll have to go catch up with him farther up the coast. Why? You guys out of money?"

Dirk snorted and Les punched him. George didn't ask any more questions. While Dirk and Les got dressed, George walked to a burger place and brought back a bag full of greasy burgers and French fries.

"Hope you got onions, Boss," Les said as they piled into the truck. "I love onions."

"Yeah, I know," George said.

He rolled down the window as they drove out of the motel parking lot and headed back to Oregon.

Chapter 10

A Sad Trip
to Santa Barbara

Tuesday, April 23rd, 5 p.m.
Santa Barbara

K im and Dr. Bolny barely caught their 12:30 flight that went nonstop to Burbank. Kim had enjoyed her conversation with Dr. Bolny on the drive to the airport. A good listener, as well as an interesting speaker, he asked about her career interests. He didn't seem to be surprised at her indecision.

"At your age, you've still got lots of time to make up your mind. I imagine you'll be good at anything you choose, so just explore everything you can and then make your choice."

On the flight down, he told her more about the gray whale and the research being done on it worldwide. Kim was so fascinated with his wealth of information, she almost wanted to take notes, but she tried to appear nonchalant as she listened to this renowned marine scientist.

They landed at Burbank at 3:22 p.m. and grabbed their bags from the overhead compartments. Kim could sense his impatience as they waited for the line of passengers in front of them to start moving. He was anxious to get to the task at hand. Once inside the terminal though, they made their way quickly to the car rental lobby. Dr. Bolny had arranged a car reservation and a brand new red Ford compact was waiting for them.

"Luckily, I've spent some time at UC Santa Barbara so I know how to get there," Dr. Bolny told her as he sped up the on ramp to the Ventura Freeway.

Kim caught her breath as they eased into the fast flowing traffic. The slow lane appeared to be doing seventy.

"We're in the going home traffic," the professor told her. "People commute as much as two hours from their jobs in L. A. But this is nothing compared to what it was like for a year after the big earthquake. I came down here for a symposium shortly after that and it took me four hours just to get across town."

"I remember that pretty well too — only a different kind of traffic. I was involved in handling emergency message traffic by ham radio," Kim told him.

Dr. Bolny asked a few questions about the many technical applications of Amateur Radio and seemed genuinely interested in Kim's answers. Soon, they were beyond the suburbs of L. A. and driving along through scenic Camarillo and Ventura. Dr. Bolny went directly to the University of California and checked in with his friend, Dr. Harris.

"There's not a lot of daylight left," Dr. Harris said, eyeing the clock, which read 6:15, "but I know you probably would like to see the whale. My wife and I are going to take you out to dinner later. Wish we had room for you at our house but we have a foreign student staying in the extra bedroom. I made arrangements for you at the dorm."

Dr. Bolny seemed not to hear the part about the social arrangements. His mind was focused on the whale. Riding in the back of Dr. Harris's jeep, Kim tried to prepare herself mentally for the sight that lay ahead. They drove into the beach parking area. A large crowd of sight-seers was gathered, partially blocking the view of the whale.

Orange ropes cordoned off the area, guarded by university students serving as security, but Kim scarcely saw them as she got out of the jeep and followed Dr. Bolny toward the dead mammal.

She knew from her studies that adult gray whales measured fifty feet long, but she hadn't quite imagined how big that really was. The huge gray animal lay on her side in the sand, a circle of flies hovering above it in the warm spring air. Dr. Bolny walked completely around it and then crouched by the head.

"Female — old, maybe forty years plus. In fact, I think this marking on her head matches some in file photos I have. I think this may be a whale that fishermen have nicknamed 'Moon.'"

Kim looked at the scene in front of her. The humans examining the whale seemed so small in comparison and yet they had the capability of deciding whether the species would live or die. She was thankful that she lived in a time when most humans tried their best to save whales. But what had killed this one? How many more were going to die?

* * *

Wednesday, April 24th, 7 a.m.
Santa Barbara

Instinctively, Kim knew Dr. Bolny would be back down at the beach at sunrise. They were booked on an afternoon flight home and he would want to use every minute he had. She got up at five, dressed, and waited in the dorm lobby.

He smiled as he saw her.

"Great minds think alike, I guess — come on, let's go."

Dr. Harris had left his jeep for them to use, saying he would join them later after an 8 o'clock lecture he had to give. It was a beautiful spring morning in the coastal community of Goleta, just north of Santa Barbara. Kim inhaled the brisk air, fragrant with eucalyptus. She wished that the drive to the beach was longer so she could savor the loveliness of the day before confronting death again. But they were soon there.

A halo of seagulls circling the dead whale marked its position. Dr. Bolny parked the jeep under a palm tree. Two students still stood guard at the perimeter of the cordoned area, but the only other human life on the beach this early was a group of surfers lying on their boards out beyond the waves.

One of the security students batted angrily at a gull, which swooped down toward the gaping hole on the whale's head. The marine biologists had already decided that the hole was the work of a Great White shark — it looked as if he had taken one huge bite and then moved on. Kim watched as Dr. Bolny looked with fascination at the opening in the whale's head.

He handed Kim a pair of rubber gloves.

"I took some tissue and blood samples yesterday, but I'd like to see what's in that hole — probably nothing remarkable, but this is the least decomposed whale that's come ashore so let's take a look."

Kim slipped the gloves on and knelt in the sand beside Dr. Bolny, holding a flashlight for him. The odor from the dead animal was intense. She could understand why the public health people were anxious that it be buried as soon as possible. A backhoe would be there at noon — about the same time they were heading to the airport.

Dr. Bolny had his hand in the open wound up to his forearm. He gave up trying to see anything with a flashlight and closed his eyes, obviously feeling for something. Kim watched curiously, almost forgetting about the odor.

He let out a small grunt, pulling back with his hand.

Kim waited for him to speak.

"There's something in there stuck right in a bony crevice. Right behind the eye socket. If my fingers were smaller, I think I could hook my forefinger behind it and pull it out. It's probably a bone fragment, but it feels awfully smooth."

"Here, let me try."

Kim pushed up the sleeve of her gray sweatshirt and pushed her hand gingerly through the dead tissue. Dr. Bolny watched the depth of her arm and gave her directions.

"That's it — straight in — now a little to your right. Do you feel the lower part of the eye socket?"

"I think so."

"Now move your fingers behind the ridge."

Yes, there was something there. A small cylindrical object. Kim grasped it with her thumb and forefinger and pulled as hard as she could. Suddenly it popped loose and she almost fell backward in the sand.

"Got it!"

She opened her palm and the two of them stared down at a bullet.

"That's what I was afraid of," Dr. Bolny said softly. "Looks like a slug from a high powered rifle — probably a 30-06. I think the lab here can run a ballistics check on it. Actually, I doubt this is the one that killed it — not in the right place. The lethal slug is probably farther in, but I doubt we could get to it without doing a complete cutdown on the animal, and I know we don't have time."

He looked down at their blood-stained hands and arms.

"I thought you mentioned a virus," Kim said.

"Well, anything is possible, but usually a virus would take its greatest toll on weak animals. This is the first old whale we've seen. The other four have been prime specimens — two young males and two young females. No, this is the work of some madman at sea."

"Why would anyone do anything like this? I mean, they're not even using the whale once they kill it."

"I don't know, Kim. There are some people who like to kill just for the sake of killing. Don't ask me to understand them — they're beyond my comprehension."

For the next hour, the two of them took photos of the whale from various angles. Kim washed the bullet in the sea water and put it on a white towel for Dr. Bolny to photograph. They would be leaving it in Santa Barbara for analysis, but he wanted photographic evidence to take home with him.

Dr. Harris arrived with some other students just as they were putting away the camera.

"You were always a good sleuth," he said after Dr. Bolny had shared his findings, "but I'm sorry this is the conclusion. Until somebody catches this person or persons, there will probably be more."

"I don't think there's a lot more we can do here, Kim," Dr. Bolny said.

"Perhaps, you'd like to go back and tour the marine biology labs," suggested Dr. Harris. "We're pretty proud of our setup."

Kim nodded yes, but before following the men back to the parking lot, she crouched down by the whale's massive head. Tiny barnacles clung to its gray skin giving it its characteristic mottled appearance. She reached out and brushed some flies away from its open eye.

"Somebody will do something about this. I promise you," she said fervently.

Gathering up her notes, she ran to join the professors.

Chapter 11

San Francisco

Wednesday, April 24th, noon
San Francisco Bay

Freddie waited patiently in line with the other crew members for customs officials to okay their two-day stay in San Francisco. He preferred the smaller ports where officials were less likely to show up, but San Francisco had its share of attractions that were worth the hassle of showing his papers. The captain didn't really care what they did as long as they didn't get arrested and were ready to sail when the ship was unloaded.

This was their largest cargo stop of the run. They were bringing a load of exotic hardwoods, which were prized by furniture and musical instrument makers. In turn, they would load on redwood and take it to Longview, Washington. There, they would pick up an additional load of Douglas fir to haul to Vancouver.

Most trips, they went all the way to Alaska, ferrying cargo from port to port. This voyage, however, would have Vancouver, British Columbia, as the turnaround point. They would be making stops in Newport and Coos Bay on the way south and probably several more along the California coast.

The drug Cartel he worked for had left it up to Freddie to establish the delivery point for the drugs. These last two shipments had been designated for the Northwest so Newport seemed a logical place to drop them. It was too risky to actually take them into port. Freddie knew of drug smugglers who actually hollowed out some of the logs and filled them with drugs. Of course, that meant someone had to get to the logs after they were delivered in port.

No, the plan he had come up with last fall seemed to be working perfectly. This was his third delivery. He figured if he made about ten trips, he would have enough money secreted away that he could give up working forever — perhaps move out of Colombia. Drug bosses weren't too friendly to employees who quit.

He could understand that. He worried about his own "employees." He trusted his old buddy, George, but the two yokels he'd picked up to help him seemed like liabilities. He'd never actually met them, but from what George told him of their antics, he wasn't impressed. Still, he guessed they were all necessary to the operation.

"You have to have a cover," he'd emphasized to George. "Each of you needs a part time job so you're not perceived as bums."

George did some maintenance work off and on, but he had no permanent residence. According to George, Dirk and Les were even less stable. They had drifted from cannery to fishery jobs for the last ten years. Every time they got a little money in their pocket, they quit and moved on. George said both of them were living in Coos Bay when he met them while making one of his first deliveries.

George emphasized to Freddie that he'd had a terrible time making the pickup at sea by himself. Lacking anywhere to stash them, he'd simply brought the drugs back to the motel. Fearing the maid would find the bundles, he'd stowed them in his truck and driven around nervously for two months until they were all gone. After he'd gotten to know Les and Dirk, he told them of his dilemma.

"No problem," Les said. "I grew up in Yachats, south of Newport. My dad and I used to fish. I know every nook and cranny of that coast line. In fact, I bet I know a cave right north of Newport that would be perfect. Hard for the average person to get into but not too hard for us."

And so the working relationship had been formed out of mutual need. Freddie hoped it would continue to go well, and if it didn't, he hoped their errors wouldn't lead back to him.

When the customs procedures were over, he walked through the docks and up the street. Most of the crew headed for Fisherman's Wharf or Chinatown for some typical San Francisco food. The diet aboard the freighter got a little monotonous at times. Freddie didn't care. What he ate was forgotten the minute he swallowed it. Food had long lost its ability to satisfy him. Alcohol halfway soothed the demons within him, but right now, he could really use something stronger than alcohol.

Someday he knew he would go back to regular use of cocaine or perhaps even heroin. More than once, he was tempted to open one of his precious bundles in the hold. Like the creatures in his dreams, there was no denying its call, but fear had its call too, and he was afraid of what would happen if he delivered an incomplete load.

For now, he would try to entertain himself in San Francisco, the city by the bay that was so full of hills. He remembered his first trip there as a child and riding on the cable cars. Now, Freddie didn't want to go anywhere near the tourist areas. He caught a bus that would drop him off in what most people called the "bad section of town." He knew several bars that served extra-stiff drinks, and in the back rooms there was usually a high stakes card game going. He patted the money in his left pocket. He felt lucky today.

* * *

Wednesday, April 24th, 4 p.m.
Portland, Oregon

Kim hadn't realized how tired she was from the excitement of the last two days. She woke up with a start just as the plane touched down in Portland and smiled as she realized that Dr. Bolny had been awakened by the landing too.

He smiled back.

"As I said, great minds think alike, but now we're going to defy one of the laws of physics which says bodies at rest..."

"....tend to stay at rest," Kim finished, yawning and laughing.

70

She stood up and stretched as much as she could in the cramped aisle and waited for the passengers to deplane. Dr. Bolny was right behind her. Once inside the terminal, they walked quickly through the crowds out to where the shuttle bus would take them to the parking lot.

"Glad you went?" he asked her after they had gotten a hamburger and were heading south to Newport.

"Yes. Yes, I am. It was sad to see that whale. Somehow just working with isolated bones and even with that entire skull we have back at the lab still didn't give me the impression of what they're really like up close. I won't ever forget how that dead gray whale looked ... and I hope I don't ever see another," she added softly.

"I know how you feel, Kim. Whenever I go to help at a mass stranding, I am always struck by the tremendous emotions that flow from the people who try to save the animals. Sometimes when we've been working all night and the animal dies, it's almost too much to bear. But those are cases that we don't understand. We know darned well what killed this gray, and most likely, the others too."

They drove on through the night — down I-5 to Highway 34 to Corvallis and on to the coast. As they passed through the quiet college town, Kim wondered what Marc was doing. On impulse, she reached into her bag and pulled out her two-meter rig.

"KA7SJP monitoring," she said after she punched up the local repeater.

"Hi Kim. KA7ITR here."

Dr. Bolny turned to look at Kim who seemed flustered, but she soon regained her composure.

"Hi Marc. Say hello to Dr. Bolny — we're just driving back to Newport from the airport. There was a dead gray that washed ashore in Santa Barbara."

"And you went down there? Oh, excuse me. Hello, Dr. Bolny."

Marc's voice sounded full of curiosity and tension.

"I wondered where you were. I tried to call you at the Marine Science Center this morning."

"Oh?"

"Yeah, just wanted to talk. By the way, your little brother called me."

"Brandon?"

"I don't think you have any others."

Kim tensed at his sarcasm.

"Oh, what did he want?" she asked, trying to keep her voice even.

"Just had a computer question — no big deal. I hope I helped him. So as I started to say, I'd like to get together to talk to you."

"I'd like that — just set a time."

"I'll call you, okay?"

"Okay. KA7ITR from KA7SJP. Clear."

They were in Philomath now and drifting out of range. The small rubber "ducky" antenna on Kim's handheld wouldn't carry very far.

He said good-bye and then something else, but his reply was too garbled to hear.

"Friend of yours?"

"Yeah. A good friend, I hope."

Dr. Bolny didn't question her, and they drove on in silence.

* * *

Thursday, April 25th, midnight
San Francisco Harbor

Freddie had lost almost all of his money and his head ached from the liquor he'd consumed. Most of the previous day and night were a blur. There was a brief memory of some woman he had tried to pick up in a bar. She'd told him to get lost in no uncertain terms.

He stopped at a public phone booth near the base of the dock. His contact in Portland would be waiting for confirmation of their itinerary. Freddie told him they would be in Newport sometime on the 27th. The contact should let George know.

The steamer was all loaded up and ready to sail in a few hours. Freddie walked up the gangplank, sipping a cup of coffee to clear his head. He would be needed at his navigator's post — perhaps he could catch a couple of hours sleep first.

Depression and then anger settled over him as he thought of the events of the last day and night. He wished they were out at sea — out at sea where he could shoot at whales. That might make him feel better.

Chapter 12

Visits with Friends

Thursday, April 25th, 10 a.m.
Monterey, California

A lisa and her mother had looked forward to their visit to the beautiful aquarium at Monterey Bay for weeks. It was one of their favorite places to go. Alisa was five, and her mother told her she would take her and her best friend Lindsay there for the day. They would tour the aquarium, have a picnic on the beach, and maybe stop for ice cream before going home.

As the three of them walked from the parking lot toward the entrance, they noticed a group of people standing near a wall, looking out to sea with binoculars, and pointing. Alisa's mother followed the direction of their gaze. There, barely one hundred yards offshore, was a mother whale and her baby.

"Grays," said one man.

"I've never seen them this close," said another man.

Alisa and Lindsay jumped up and down in excitement as the baby whale spouted alongside his mother and then the two of them dove downward, their tails shimmering in the sunlight.

Silver Star's mother rested for a moment while her baby nuzzled close and drank the rich milk from her body. It was true — they were closer to shore than they had been. Whether it was by accident or whether the unique sonar communication of marine mammals told her that Moon had died, something made her want to stay away from the migration lanes she normally shared with passing ships.

The waters were rich here off this northern California peninsula — but not as rich as the Arctic ahead of them. As

steadily as a precision clock, her brain told her that they were behind schedule.

It was good to rest for a moment while Silver Star fed, but then she needed to speed back up. If she stopped to eat here, they would never reach the Arctic in time for the summer explosion of krill and other microorganisms that provided their nutritious diet. She broke the surface with her huge head and Silver Star tried to imitate her.

"Look at that!" Alisa cried happily. "She's sitting up!"

"That's called spy hopping," the man next to them explained. "People aren't quite sure why they do it — perhaps to get a better look at the land or maybe to hear the sounds above water."

"Hi whales!" Lindsay yelled.

"Bye whales," Alisa called as the two plunged downward again and then surfaced at an angle going out to sea.

"Have a safe trip," said Alisa's mother. "Come on girls. Let's go see the aquarium."

* * *

Thursday, April 25th, noon
Corvallis, Oregon

In a small coffee shop at the outskirts of campus, Marc sat having lunch with his longtime buddy, Ken. Ken had graduated last year in computer science and was working in Portland, but he was off for a few days and had given Marc a call to see if he was free for lunch.

"I don't have a lab until two so no hurry. So how have you been? How do you like working for a living?" Marc asked as they ate their sandwiches.

"The money's great, but the weekends are a bummer. I live in an apartment complex east of town and so far my social life has been zilch. It's mostly guys in my apartment, and by the time I get home at night, I'm beat. My life is about as exciting as my parents'. I work, I come home, I make dinner, I watch TV, and then I go to bed. On weekends, I do my laundry."

Marc laughed but looked at his friend sympathetically. "My social life's not too hot these days either."

"You're kidding? Whatever happened to your radio maiden, Kim? I thought you two were inseparable."

"That's what I'd like to think too, and I made the mistake — big mistake — of telling that to Kim. So now she thinks I'm pressuring her to get married and she's really backed off."

"Were you?"

"Well, I didn't think so. It's just that she's so busy. And I guess to be honest that's one of the things I like about her. She's interested in everything — always off on some research project or new activity. In fact this term, she's working at the Marine Science Center in Newport.

"I talked to her last night for about two minutes. She had just gotten back from Santa Barbara. Investigating the death of a gray whale. I didn't even know she had gone down there. Like I said — we're not exactly in close touch these days."

Marc paused and swirled the ice in his glass of soda pop.

"And you feel left out. Yeah you do; come on admit it." Marc half smiled.

"Exactly what did you say to Kim? Did you ask her to marry you?"

"Well, not in those words. I just wanted some sort of commitment — some way of knowing that when she's running all over the place that she belongs to me."

"Belongs? That's a bad word, Marc. How can anyone belong to anyone?"

"Yeah, I know."

"What are you — twenty-two?"

"Twenty-one — almost twenty-two. I'm a senior, but I'm in a five-year program so I won't graduate for another year."

"And Kim?"

"She's nineteen — she'll be twenty next summer. She's a sophomore. And all the different graduate programs she's talking about — well, I wouldn't be surprised if she's in school for another five years."

"And you expect her to make a lifelong decision now?"

"Gee, you make me sound like some kind of creep or something."

"No offense, buddy. It just sounds to me like you're asking her to say something she's not ready to say. She seemed like a really great girl to me. I think you need to be careful or you'll scare her away."

"I probably already have," Marc said miserably.

* * *

Thursday, April 25th, 6 p.m.
Lincoln City

"Well sure, Mom, I'd love to have dinner with all of you," Kim had told her mother when she called earlier in the afternoon. "Yes, I know, I haven't been in touch. Just been busy. Do you want to come down here? Wait a minute — why don't we meet halfway? Doesn't Dad get off at five? I'll meet you at the Sea Breeze at six in Lincoln City."

So now the four of them sat in the ocean front restaurant. Brandon had just gotten his driver's permit and was entertaining everyone with his experience coming over to the coast.

"Like there's a car a mile ahead of me on the road and Mom starts screaming SLOW DOWN! WE'LL ALL BE KILLED! I swear she about slammed her foot through the floorboard trying to put on that imaginary brake of hers."

"I did not, Brandon," Mrs. Stafford complained.

"Yes, you did, dear," laughed her husband.

"Wait until you have children, Brandon. Then you'll understand," his mother said.

They ordered dinner and chatted about everything from Kim's work at the lab to the condition of their neighbor in Salem who had just had heart surgery. Brandon was the first to bring up the real reason for their visit.

"So what have you done to Marc? I asked him about you, when he stopped by last week on his way home to visit his parents, and he acted real funny like. Have you gone and done some stupid female thing? Marc's a neat guy."

"Brandon...." his mother warned.

There was silence at the table. Finally, Kim spoke.

"No, Brandon, I haven't done some stupid female thing as you put it, and by the way, I really resent that. I know I didn't tell you any of this before, but Marc and I kind of had a parting of the ways at the end of last term. We just see our relationship differently — that's all."

"You're still friends, aren't you?" her father asked.

"Yeah, I think so. In fact, I think we're going to get together this weekend."

Kim didn't tell them about the unhappy meeting they had already had at the coast. She really didn't want to talk about it all, but she knew her family regarded Marc practically as a member. Brandon was never happier than when Marc came to visit. She sighed and changed the topic.

"Did I tell you I stuck my arm clear up to my armpit in a dead whale's head?" she asked Brandon.

"You did? Really?"

She knew he loved gory stories, so she laid it on thick as she described the recent trip to Santa Barbara and the examination of the dead whale.

"So do they have any idea who's killing them?" her father asked.

"Not yet, but everyone is working on it."

"Everyone? Oh Kim, don't tell me you're getting involved in something involving shooting," her mother said, a note of fear in her voice.

"Don't worry, Mom — all I did was pass the information along to the local ham radio club and to some of the maritime nets."

Mrs. Stafford didn't look satisfied. She knew her daughter too well not to suspect that she might try to solve the mystery herself. They visited a while longer, and then walked out to the parking lot.

"Another early day, tomorrow," Kim told them. "I guess I had better get back. And you've got school too," she said punching Brandon playfully in the arm.

They hugged good-bye and Kim laughed as Brandon got in on the driver's side.

"Keep it under ninety!" she yelled to him as they rolled out of the lot.

Chapter 13

White Powder: Gray Death

Thursday April 25th, 11 p.m.
Portland, Oregon

Bud Liles, manager of BB's Night Club, yelled for Wylie his assistant. Chuck Tatan, age 45, president of a local shipping firm that dealt exclusively with the Orient, lay unconscious, barely breathing, on the restroom floor.

"What do we do?" he asked Wylie.

"First thing we do is get rid of the evidence."

Wylie scooped up the dollar bill with the residue of white powdered cocaine still on it. He tossed it in a toilet and flushed it.

"Now call 911. You tell them you came in here to use the restroom and found this guy on the floor."

Wylie continued to give his boss instructions.

"Then you make sure the stuff's well hidden — you know in the usual place. Anybody else with him when this happened?"

"I don't think so — sounds like things are really hopping in the bar. He bought the powder from me less than fifteen minutes ago. I told him — just like I always tell our backroom customers — not to use it here."

"Yeah, well I guess he didn't listen."

Bud Liles called an ambulance while Wylie sat with the unconscious man. He was grateful the man was still breathing. The idea of trying to do CPR on someone repulsed him. Bud Liles came back in, saying the emergency crew would be there soon.

Liles took over from Wylie so that he could go out in the bar. He circulated among the patrons, telling them that someone had apparently had a heart attack in the restroom and not to be alarmed when the ambulance arrived. He knew that at least three other customers were carrying bags of cocaine, recently purchased in the backroom from his boss. People with drugs tended to get nervous when they heard sirens. At the news, a few of them chose to leave.

Chuck Tatan was turning a dusky blue and twitching. Bud Liles kept shaking his shoulder.

"Hey, come on — wake up!"

The ambulance attendants burst through the door. Immediately, they slapped an oxygen mask on the man and began taking his vital signs.

"Blood pressure 80 over 40."

"He's stopped breathing!"

Frantically, they bent over him, trying to revive him. Bud Liles stood up and walked into the bar. He was sweating profusely, and the noise of the customers seemed deafening.

"Are you the manager?"

"Yes, yes I am."

"I'm going to need to ask you some questions."

Liles turned to go over to a small table with the police officer who had stopped him.

"Not much I can tell you. I know who that guy is — name's Chuck Tatan. He comes in here a couple of times a week. Usually drinks beer and sits by himself over on that side of the room."

He gestured toward the south side of the bar.

"Tonight, I had to use the restroom — I usually go in there every hour or so anyway just to make sure nothing needs tidying up, and here he is lying on the floor. The bartender says he'd been gone about twenty minutes."

"You have any reason to believe this man might have been using drugs of any sort?"

Bud Liles felt his hands grow clammy.

"No. Why?"

"Oh, just the way he looked. I've seen a lot of cases — can't be sure, but we'll check it out."

"You think he's going to recover?"

At the moment, the restroom door opened, and another police officer came out. He came over to their table.

"He's dead. They're still trying, but he's dead."

It was over an hour before all the emergency personnel were gone. The dead man, hooked to equipment, had been transported to the hospital. After cordoning off the restroom for the crime lab to inspect, the officers stayed behind to question people. Finally they left.

Shaking from the incident, Bud Liles walked to the kitchen and drew himself a large glass of water.

"You think they'll trace it?" he asked Wylie who was nibbling on a leftover sandwich.

"Oh, they'll figure out it's cocaine all right, but they can't know how long he'd had it in him. By the way, Boss. Our supplies are running low. When do we get another shipment?"

"Next week. I called our man in Portland today."

* * *

Friday, April 26th, 9 a.m.
Newport, Oregon

"So what can be done about this?" a student questioned Dr. Bolny as he and Kim showed the last of the slides taken in Santa Barbara.

"We're not positive this isn't an isolated incident," Dr. Bolny said. "This is the only gray whale from which anyone has recovered a bullet. However, the others were far more decomposed when they washed ashore, and no one did much probing. It is our educated guess that all of the whales were killed by the same person or persons. We've notified the Coast Guard to be on the lookout for anyone firing at whales, and Kim took some other steps. Perhaps, she'd like to share them with you."

Kim walked up the steps to the podium and took the microphone.

"I guess by now most of you know I'm a ham radio operator," she said. "Well, Amateur Radio operators have what they call 'nets,' short for networks. That's a time when all operators who have something in common gather on the same frequency and talk to each other. There are nets for retired teachers, for missionaries — you name it. There are also several maritime nets. Those are nets where people at sea talk. They often pass emergency messages for one another or simply relay information home.

"This morning, I checked in with one at 8 a.m. that meets on twenty meters. I talked to a WB6BYU who is sailing up the coast of Oregon to Vancouver with his family. I told him a little of what happened and he said he would watch. Better yet, he'll pass the information to other maritime nets so we reach everyone who's a ham off the coast.

"Another ham, W7BKU, actually came back to me from the air. He's a pilot who takes people on sight-seeing tours especially to whale watch. He offered to keep a lookout."

"You don't think someone's going to shoot a whale with people watching, do you?" a girl in the back row asked.

"Probably not," Dr. Bolny interjected. "But stranger things have happened. If this person is bold enough to break the law, then he may be bold enough to do it right in front of someone. At any rate, the more eyes we have watching, the better chance of success. The whale-watching charter boat operators have also been alerted. It's against the law to come closer than one hundred yards of a gray whale, so they're going to watch for violations of that."

The students listened attentively, often murmuring among themselves. After the lecture, they gathered in the lobby before returning to their various labs. Kim, Julie and Megan sat on the ledge by the "petting tidepool." Signs instructing visitors how to gently handle the sea urchins, anenomes and other creatures were posted on the wall. Another sign posted on the octopus tank warned of the importance of touching the octopus carefully and of not pulling away suddenly, lest he be injured.

"Quite a contrast, isn't it?" Megan said sadly. "We try to teach people not to hurt the sea anemones and then there's someone out there blasting holes in whales."

"Remember when there was a run on killing sharks off Southern California, years ago?" Julia asked.

"Yeah, I think I do," Kim said. "Some club was actually having contests to see how many of them people could kill — blues were worth so many points, nurse sharks so many, and, of course, Great Whites were the top prize. I remember seeing photos of people holding up their trophies."

"Do they still have those contests?"

"I haven't seen anything in the news about it lately; have you?" Kim asked Megan.

"No, I would hope some of the documentaries on television showing how sharks contribute to the ecological balance of the sea have helped."

"You've got a lot more faith in mankind than I do then," said Julia. "More than likely, it was just a fad that ran its course. Don't be surprised if it comes back."

"Boy, aren't you the cynic," Megan said.

"No, I'm a realist."

On that note, the girls parted and went to their lab assignments. In the bone lab, a necropsy (autopsy on an animal) was underway. A dead sea lion had been found by the mouth of the bay.

"Did someone shoot that too?" Kim asked Chris, a graduate student.

"Wouldn't be the first one. The salmon fishermen are getting pretty upset with losing part of their catch to these animals. Some of them would like to kill seals to save the salmon."

"The world's getting crazy," said Kim. "What kind of a balance is it if we have to kill one animal to save another?"

"There are two sides to that argument," Chris reminded her.

"I know, I know."

Kim looked at the beautiful sleek animal spread out on the dissecting table. She had seen seals and sea lions dissected before and had never gotten over the size of their lungs. No wonder they could stay underwater so long and swim so fast. Their bodies were literally containers for air and muscle.

"No bullets here," Chris said. "It looks like a fairly old animal and the lungs appear congested. It may have had some sort of respiratory illness."

When Chris and two other students took a break for lunch, Kim remained behind in the lab. She wanted some time alone to think about her surprise for Dr. Bolny. The students had talked about a surprise party for his May 5th birthday. Carefully, she removed the cloth from the whale's head on the floor and studied it. An idea was coming to her. It would involve both of her two-meter radios and some parts that she could probably buy in town. She really wanted to surprise everyone, so that meant she would have to work on it when they weren't around.

The afternoon flew by. As Kim closed her notebook at 4:30, she was amazed at the notes she had gathered. For a beginning marine science student, she was certainly being exposed to research. And it was all fascinating. Maybe this was her area. But then she remembered the children at the hospital at Portland — working in the medical field helping kids appealed to her too. Kim sighed. At least, she knew that she had narrowed her major to the biological sciences — helping animals or people, but at this point she wasn't sure which.

She was daydreaming about all of this as she walked down the hall and straight into Jack.

"Whoa — are you in a daze or what?"

"Oh! Yeah, I guess I am. Sorry. How did your day go?"

"Long. But my paper is coming along pretty well. I just realized I skipped lunch and I'm starved. How about you?"

"Now that you mention it," Kim laughed, rubbing her stomach.

"Want to go find some more exceptional crab or superb clam chowder? Also I'd like to hear more about your experiences in Santa Barbara."

"Sold," Kim said. "But let's find some cheap exceptional crab or chowder. I'm kind of broke."

"This one's on me," said Jack.

"No, we go Dutch or I won't go."

Jack shook his head and smiled. Kim had very definite ideas about everything.

"Okay — whatever. I promise I won't even open any doors for you."

"But I like that," Kim laughed.

She ran upstairs to put away her books and change her clothes. It was still chilly in the evenings, so she slipped a warm cable-knit white sweater over her blue turtleneck and jeans.

"Where you off to in such a rush?" Julia asked as she rummaged through the cupboard for something to fix for dinner.

"Jack and I are going out for a bowl of chowder. Want to come along?"

"No, no, Kim — two's company and three's a crowd. I'm not going to be in the way."

"It's not like that, Julia. Really it isn't."

Julia looked skeptical as Kim unfastened her long pony-tail and brushed her golden-brown curls vigorously.

"You ought to leave it down," Megan said, coming into the room.

"Not a chance," Kim said. "The wind blows it everywhere."

Julia and Megan exchanged glances as Kim fastened her hair back into a ponytail with a red ribbon. Kim was a hard one to figure out. They knew she'd had some sort of falling out with her boyfriend, but she never offered any details.

"Have fun," Julia yelled after her.

Chapter 14

Waiting for the Drop

Kim and Jack decided to stop and see Gary at the Coast Guard Station before having supper. Kim wanted to tell him first hand what she'd seen on the beach in Santa Barbara.

"Yeah, I got the report here that Dr. Bolny called in. I think the information has gone out up and down the coast — from the Mexican border clear up to Alaska. I wouldn't hold out too much hope of our vessels seeing anything though."

"I've put it out on the maritime nets too," Kim said.

"Maybe we'll get a lead that way."

Just then Gary was called to answer a phone call. Jack and Kim waved good-bye and walked outside.

"Why don't we just leave my car here and walk down into Old Town," Jack suggested. "It's kind of a nice night."

They made their way down the steep hill to the strip facing Yaquina Bay. Shop owners were just closing up. In the summer, they would be open later, but now six o'clock was good enough.

"Just a minute," Kim said. "My brother's birthday is next week, and I promised him I would get him salt-water taffy. Let's hurry before they close. I hope they have bubble gum — that's his favorite flavor."

It was getting dark as they walked to the end of the street, Kim carrying her bag full of taffy.

"Special — Clam Chowder — all you can eat $2.50"

"That's for me," said Kim.

"Me too — I think they're going to lose money."

The next hour and a half were spent happily eating and talking. Kim discovered she had a lot in common with Jack, but she found herself mentally comparing him with Marc. They were both nice, both smart, and they both had a wacky sense of humor. If anything, Jack probably had a more even disposition, but just thinking that made her feel disloyal to Marc. She was surprised at the intensity of feeling she still had for him.

"You're daydreaming again," Jack softly.

"I'm sorry; a lot has happened this week. I guess I was sort of going over it."

They paid their bill and left the cafe. The wind had come up and Kim shivered slightly as they walked back up the hill.

"Listen!" Jack said, taking her arm.

Kim stopped walking. The melancholy wail of the lighthouse foghorn drifted toward them.

"What? The foghorn?"

"No. Above that."

Kim held her breath, listening intently. There was a faint shrill scream in the distance.

"What is it?"

"Muriel."

"Muriel?"

Jack lowered his voice dramatically.

"You mean you've been here over a month and you haven't heard about Muriel?"

Kim shook her head no.

"Muriel Trevenard was a teenager who arrived in Newport in 1875. Her father left her and she lived with a Newport family. One night a group including Muriel visited the Yaquina Bay Lighthouse. They left through a shaft going to the rocks. Muriel went back to get a handkerchief she'd dropped.

"They waited for her but she didn't come out. Then they heard her scream," Jack said, enjoying the expression on Kim's face. "They rushed back in and found a pool of warm blood on the stairs and a blood-stained handkerchief. The iron door to the shaft had been closed."

"Ooh," shivered Kim. "Remind me never to invite you to a Halloween party. Did they ever find her?"

"Nope, but on foggy nights, you still hear her scream."

"Are you making up all this?"

"Nope, scout's honor. It's all in the historical society records."

They walked on up the hill, Kim listening for Muriel's screams, but they had faded. Suddenly Jack shouted "Lookout!" and shoved Kim into the ivy on the shoulder of the road as a pickup truck came barreling right at them.

The driver of the truck slowed as the headlights caught them in the glare. Jack shook his fist at the driver as the truck picked up speed again and continued on down the hill.

"Don't," whispered Kim.

"What?"

"I think that's the same truck that chased me back to the center the other night."

"Chased you?"

"Oh just some drunks having fun, but they scared me."

"Are you sure it's the same one?"

"Not absolutely, but I think so. The guy driving looked familiar."

"Want to go back and get their license number?"

"No, let's just go."

They drove back to the Marine Science Center. Jack started to tell her another ghost story, but Kim silenced him.

"I've had enough excitement for one night," she said truthfully.

At the center she said good-bye to Jack and walked to the back of the building where her apartment was.

"Hi," Julia greeted her, looking up from her books. "Have fun?"

"Sure. Great clam chowder — wish I knew how to make that stuff."

"Oh by the way," said Megan. "You got a call. A guy from OSU. Said he was a friend of yours. Didn't leave a message."

"Where did you tell him I was?"

"Just out having dinner with a friend."

"Did he say he'd call back?"

"No, just said good-bye and hung up."

* * *

90

Friday, April 26th, 10 p.m.
Newport, Oregon

"Well it's Little Miss Ponytail again with a boyfriend this time," laughed Dirk.

"You idiot," said George. "I knew I should never let you drive this thing. You trying to get us arrested?"

"Nope, Boss, just hungry. Want to get some fresh crab before the stores close. Remember I haven't eaten in two days."

"And whose fault is that?" laughed Les. "You're the one who had to pig down all those burgers in Spokane. Not our concern that you got sick. George and I've been just fine, eating three meals a day while you lay there begging to die. For someone who's been as green looking as you, I doubt that crab is the best meal. Probably get sick all over again."

Dirk swore. They'd pulled up in front of the seafood market, and it was closed.

"I told you it would be," said George. "Probably shut down at six."

"I wanted to buy a whole mess of them and take them back to the motel. Man, I am powerful hungry. Guess we'll have to go to that cafe instead. I just hope they have enough — way I feel now, I could eat at least a dozen."

George and Les exchanged glances.

"If you don't kill yourself of a busted gut, it'll be a miracle," George said. "Well, come on — let's go eat, but try not to be too obnoxious. In other words, try not to be yourself."

The men walked into the cafe and sat down at a corner table. They'd been in town for nearly two days now, waiting for the call giving the coordinates of the latest shipment. There had been no call, and the lumber freighter hadn't come into port. George was extremely nervous.

Although he knew the schedule for the *Si Maria* could vary, he'd been told it would come in today. Supposing the drug boss in Portland had found someone else to do his delivery work for him? Suppose he had heard of Les and Dirk's escapade in Spokane? Suppose he had assigned someone to eliminate them from the picture? He rubbed his hands together anxiously as he waited for the waitress to take their order.

Pickups of the drug drop were always at midnight. That was when the release timer attached to the bundles activated a CO_2 cartridge. The gas filled a rubber bladder that popped to the surface carrying the drugs with it. Since the ship usually came into port during the daylight hours, the bundles were dropped in the darkness hours while they waited outside the jetty.

After the ship docked, Freddie called them himself, confirming that at midnight the drugs would be on the surface for pickup. That was why it was so important that one of them be near the phone on the expected date of delivery. If no one answered, then Freddie called a higher-up in Portland or Seattle who relayed the message later. That was not good for their record as pickup men and couriers.

Freddie had a strict protocol he insisted they follow. He would never meet with George until after the drugs had been retrieved. The ship didn't always stay in port that long, but if it did, Freddie would have a celebration drink with George at two in the morning — that is, if they could find a bar that was open. That was also when Freddie handed over the money in payment for delivery of the last batch.

He had good reason for his caution. If something went wrong — if George, Les and Dirk were apprehended in the pickup process, Freddie didn't want anyone to have seen him drinking with George. If the ship left before they had a chance to meet, then perhaps he could catch George on the return trip. Of course it was possible that the ship wouldn't come into Newport at all. He had warned George of that too.

"I never know from port to port what the final itinerary will be," he'd told George. "If they change it at the last minute, I'll try to let you know."

The first two deliveries George had been involved in had gone smoothly, but now he was worried. What if the itinerary had been changed and the shipment for Newport had been rescheduled for the return trip. Or worse yet, perhaps the drop was going to be made somewhere else. Then someone else would do the pickup. George didn't want that to happen. He wanted the job and he wanted it badly. By the time their meal was brought to the table, he had worked himself into such a state, he wasn't hungry.

All afternoon, he had alternated between staying in the motel room waiting for the phone to ring and walking out to a nearby bluff to scan the horizon with binoculars. He'd seen a couple of fishing vessels but nothing that looked like a lumber steamer. Les and Dirk seemed oblivious to worries. He watched them with disdain as they dug into the plates of crab, cracking the red shells noisily and sucking out the tender morsels inside.

"What's the matter, Boss? Not hungry?"

"I have other things on my mind," George told them.

* * *

Saturday, April 27th, 1 a.m.
Near Florence

Freddie tossed and turned in his bunk. He was having dreams again. Not even a walk on the deck and a couple of shots at something he was pretty sure was a whale had relaxed him. He felt like the timing was all off kilter in his life. They were a day behind schedule due to getting out of San Francisco late. Then an unexpected storm near northern California slowed them down even more. When it was stormy, he had to spend more time at his navigator's desk, which meant he got less sleep. And, of course, when it was cloudy, there was no light for night-time hunting.

He still wasn't recovered from his binge in San Francisco — that coupled with the bad dreams and a terrible sense of foreboding tormented him as he tried to sleep. Soon it would be morning. He thought they would reach the mouth of Newport Bay about 5 a.m. Freddie needed to drop his precious bundles overboard while it was still dark, and he hoped to drop them in alignment with the point on shore that the men used for reference during the pickup. He'd spent quite a bit of time figuring the currents and how much the bundles might drift before their anchor took them to the bottom. The release timer would disconnect them from the weight that held them at the bottom.

Best of all, the handheld global positioning system he had would give him exact coordinates to tell the men, but he still worried about unknowns. What if the currents changed? What if the timer didn't work? What if someone else found the bundles? If anything went wrong — if for instance they didn't reach Newport before daylight, he would have to hold on to the shipment and try to drop it on the way back. All of this went through his brain as the ship rolled with the ocean swells.

I'll just sleep for an hour, he told himself. Then I'll get up and check our position and be ready. He turned over and closed his eyes but then opened them in terror. There were weird things inside his head — long wispy tendrils and red glowing eyes. A cavernous mouth opened as if to speak and then closed again. The tendrils reached out to him. Things in his dreams had color and clarity that his real world near-sightedness never had. Freddie jumped out of bed and threw on his clothes. Another night with just three hours of sleep. He could feel the fatigue in his bones, but he knew there would be no more sleep for him this night. He would ride out the rest of the darkness in the wheelhouse, drinking coffee, pretending to study his navigation charts, and waiting — waiting until it was time.

Chapter 15

Death in the Water

Saturday, April 27th, 6 a.m.
Newport

K im opened her eyes and looked at the fluorescent dial on her alarm clock. 6 a.m. There was no reason to get up yet. She planned on joining the maritime net at 8 a.m. just to see if there were any developments in the whale shooting case. She rolled over on her side and tried to sleep. In the distance, the barking of sea lions and the roar of crashing surf broke the morning quiet. Must be another storm brewing.

Once she was awake, she knew there was little hope of going back to sleep. She got up and walked barefoot to the small kitchen to put water on to boil for tea. Julia and Megan shared the larger bedroom in the back of the apartment.

When the tea was ready, she carried a steaming mug back to her bedroom and closed the door. Grabbing the quilted flowered comforter her mother had made for her, Kim wrapped herself in it in front of the ham rig. After donning headphones, she switched on the transceiver and quickly tuned up on twenty meters.

The band seemed dead and she smiled remembering her discussion with Jack about "deceased" frequencies.

"Maybe you are just asleep," she whispered softly as she tuned up and down the band.

A faint signal caught her attention and she adjusted her tuning to bring it in to its maximum strength.

"Mayday!" It was a distress call! She turned up the volume and concentrated on hearing through the static.

"...badly injured...150 miles southeast..."

150 miles southeast of what? Kim punched her mike button.

"This is KA7SJP to the station calling with an injured person. Say again please."

"KA7SJP — this is N7JRE. Please get in touch with authorities at Tahiti. I say again, authorities at Tahiti. We are 150 miles southeast of ... — have a badly injured fisherman. Do you copy?"

Kim forgot her sleeping roommates and practically shouted into the microphone.

"Yes, N7JRE, I copy. Tell me your location please. 150 miles southeast of what?"

Now all she could hear was static. Then a clear voice broke in.

"KA7SJP this is KB7YLA three hundred miles east of Hawaii. I copied your QSO with the station near Bora Bora, but now I've lost them. The location is 150 miles SE of Bora Bora — do you copy?"

"KB7YLA from KA7SJP. Yes, I do. Please go ahead. Do you have any further information?"

"There are two hams on board, N7JRE and her husband, N7IIR. They're sailing on a vacation and they've picked up an injured fisherman. I'm going to try to raise someone in Hawaii — will you contact the Coast Guard there in the states too?"

Kim assured her she would. She was curious to know more about all the people involved, but there was no time to waste now. She grabbed the phone and called the Newport Coast Guard. She gave all the information she had to the officer on duty. He asked her name and phone number and call letters. Quickly, she turned back to the rig.

"KB7YLA from KA7SJP."

"Go ahead KA7SJP. This is KB7YLA."

"Just wanted to tell you that I have contacted the Coast Guard and the message will be passed on. Thank you again for relaying."

"Oh, you're welcome. Thank you!"

Her voice sounded young so on an impulse, Kim asked her how old she was.

"I'm just curious if you're my age. I'm a student at the Marine Science Center here and am 19."

The girl laughed.

"Not quite — just turning fifteen this summer. I'm out of school for two weeks sailing to Hawaii with my uncle KD7KD and my aunt KB7YKZ. My parents and my brother are along too. We're having a great time."

Kim was anxious to hear more details, but the band was truly fading. She signed and promised KB7YLA that she'd send her a QSL card. She sounded like the kind of person she'd like to keep in touch with.

Last summer in the lookout tower, she had been the vital link for someone at sea, and now here it was happening again. The thought of strangers reaching out through radio waves clear across the world and helping each other made her shiver with excitement. She left the ham radio on while she dressed.

The other girls were just getting up as Kim finished her ritual bowl of oatmeal. They shook their heads in disbelief as they saw she was fully dressed.

"Don't you ever sleep in?" Megan yawned.

"Not very often," Kim admitted. "Excuse me, the net should be starting — I want to hear if anything's happened with the whales or if the Coast Guard has found that boat near Tahiti."

"Tahiti?" Julia asked, but Kim had already gone back to her bedroom.

* * *

Saturday, April 27th, 9:00 a.m.
North of San Francisco

The morning sun sent shimmers of gold across the blue-gray Pacific Ocean as flecks of foam swirled the colors together. Several hundred yards east on shore, heavy mist hanging over the lush redwood forests also sparkled in the early sunlight. It was as if everything including the ocean had been washed clean. The rain of the previous night had ceased and now tiny rivulets of water made their way through the bough-covered forest floor. The water joined streams and flowed west into the ocean.

For Silver Star and his mother, the rich taste of soil and bark mingled with the other ocean flavors. A vast array of sensory data was being stored in Silver Star's brain. On his next trip, he would remember these smells and tastes — would correlate them with his position on the coast and know whether he was where he should be according to the internal time clock that drove him.

Suddenly, his mother veered from their path close to the shoreline. Following her trustingly, he trailed her as she headed farther out to sea. Why? His young senses were on the alert. There was a strange unpleasant odor that made him afraid. He didn't understand it and it was new to him. His mother swam faster, and he sensed her fear, too. They went almost a half mile off course as she kept up the faster pace for nearly an hour. Finally, his mother slowed so he could nurse.

He had no idea what it was they had avoided or swum from. He had seen nothing more than the familiar blue-gray waters and his mother's reassuring gray bulk. Silver Star's mother hadn't actually seen anything either, but she had sensed it and that was enough. Death was in the waters behind her. A young mother gray whale and her baby were both dead, floating in the current. Sharks were feeding on their decomposing bodies. By the time they drifted ashore, there would be little left.

She cut their resting period short and swam on. They must get to the Arctic.

* * *

Saturday, April 27th, noon
Newport Harbor

"It's there," was the way Freddie began his brief call to George. "Up at midnight as usual. And we're sailing around three, so guess I'll miss you. We'll be back around the second or third. I'll give you your payment then."

George started to protest but realized it was useless. When it came to payment, he had to do it the way Freddie said and just be grateful, even though it was an unusual way for a drug courier to be paid.

"Okay," George said. "But you'd better not miss us on the way back. We've done all the deliveries right on schedule. My boys don't like to be put off."

Freddie laughed.

"You'll get paid — don't worry."

Then he gave him the exact coordinates from his GPS (Global Positioning System) and they both hung up. Freddie looked around before stepping out of the phone booth on the dock. He was used to looking over his shoulder before he did anything. He glanced out to sea under the bridge and through the rock jetties. He even shaded his eyes with his hand as though he could see through the jetties and to the kelp bed a half mile south of the bay.

It was there while the ship waited for daylight to dock, that he had thrown the cocaine bundles overboard. They sank immediately. Freddie hoped they wouldn't drift too much before hitting bottom. At midnight, the release timer attached to them would automatically activate the CO^2 and detach the anchor weight. A second timer would start a small flashing strobe light so that the bundles would be easily visible. If George, Les and Dirk were where they were supposed to be, there would be no problem.

"Whatcha lookin at?"

Freddie jumped at his crew member's voice.

"Oh nothing," he said uneasily. "Just looking to see if there's a storm coming in. Weather forecast said there was."

"Seems like there's always a storm coming or going in this part of the country. Want to go get some lunch?"

Freddie declined. Joseph was one of the few crew members who spoke fluent English, but Freddie made it a point not to get too close to anyone. Friendships invited questions, and questions were the last thing he wanted.

"Naw, I'm not feeling too well," Freddie said, rubbing his hand over his forehead. "I may just get a nap before we sail."

Joseph clapped his shoulder good-naturedly and joined a couple of his buddies who were heading into town. Freddie went into a corner market, bought a loaf of bread and some smoked salmon, and returned to his bunk to eat it. The ship was silent except for the creaking of rigging as it swayed on the swells in the harbor. Even the captain had gone ashore. The load for Newport was a small one and it would be unloaded at 1 p.m. He'd heard the Captain talking that they might be bringing back a larger load on the return trip.

With his stomach full, he dozed off to sleep. This time there were no dreams.

Chapter 16

Bundles in a Cave
and Pins on a Map

Saturday, April 27th 11:30 p.m.
Just south of Newport

C arrying the rubber Zodiac runabout above their heads, the three men dressed in black wetsuits bent against the wind as they climbed down the rocky surface. George was in the lead and he scrambled over the slippery rocks directly below the stand of shore pine on the cliff. With Les helping, he put the boat in the water. The three of them pushed the craft and then George and Les scrambled in while Dirk kept guiding it until he was chest deep. They helped him over the edge into the boat.

Getting through the surf was treacherous and the men almost capsized, but true to his word, Les was a good skipper. He sat in the rear by the outboard engine and held the course of the small craft steady as they headed due west beyond the breaker line.

Thanks to the advances of modern technology, they also had a miniature GPS system that told them exactly where they were on the Earth's surface. Years before, such devices were unheard of. Now anyone with a few hundred bucks could buy one. Military experts constantly worried that terrorists would use the devices to deliver payloads of explosives to exact locations. The GPS was extraordinarily accurate. Now all the men had to do was line up with the coordinates Freddie had given them over the phone. George held the fluorescent face of the GPS up close in the darkness and called out directions to Les, who steered the boat effortlessly. It was their aim to be right at the drop point before the bundles bobbed to the surface.

The shoreline soon became invisible in the night and the rain. The coordinates Freddie had given them were almost identical to those of last time, which meant the drop point was roughly equidistant from two buoys, forming the easternmost point of a triangle. At 11:55, the men were in position. At precisely midnight, several bundles encased in green waterproof plastic shot to the surface so close to the boat that Dirk jumped. He reached over the side and turned off the blinking strobe light before hauling them aboard.

"Last time we had to drive around for nearly an hour before we found it — guess this is our lucky night," George yelled over the wind.

The men stacked the packages in the boat, grateful for the stormy weather and the darkness that shielded them from land. At a street value of $50,000 a kilo, their small boat held a potential cargo of two and a half million dollars. George threw a tarp over the drug bundles.

Now came the dangerous part. The cave where they hid the stuff was north of the bay, which meant they had to pilot their boat right across the mouth of the bay. But there were no boats out at this hour, and their passage went unnoticed.

By 12:30 a.m., they had maneuvered close to shore and into the mouth of the cave. Les held the boat steady against the rocks while George and Dirk, armed with flashlights, swam the stuff into the cave. It was high tide and the rock shelf where they tied their precious booty was barely above the water line. Working as quickly as they could, they stowed it and then swam back to the boat. Now all that was left was to make it back across the mouth of the bay and down to the rocky beach where they had put in.

On subsequent retrievals, they could launch their boat closer to the cave, but tonight they'd had to be close to the drug drop. Despite their wetsuits, all three men were shivering by the time they got back to the beach and lugged the deflated boat up the embankment. Grateful for the protection of the trees, the three of them stripped and changed into regular clothes before getting back in the truck.

"You smell worse than a wet dog," George complained as the truck heater roared into force and Dirk struggled into a grimy sweatshirt. "Don't you ever bathe?"

"Hey Boss, I just went swimming. What's the complaint?" Les chuckled.

"Make that a doggone rich wet dog, Boss. Dirk and me have been talking about taking on a little more culture — we going back to Spokane any time soon? We got a beef we wanta settle with one snooty waiter."

"Not that I know of you two, and if you go getting into any fights, you're out of this operation. Is that understood?"

"Yeah, Boss but I don't think you ever have any fun."

George was silent. He had his own plans for the money. He already had over two hundred thousand hidden away from less than six months work. And Freddie had told him it might pick up in the summer months. Why, he might even go down to Colombia and visit Freddie — maybe there was more money to be made at that end. His idea of fun was to be able to do nothing for the rest of his life.

"Any bars open?" George asked. "I feel like a drink."

"Nope," said Dirk, "but this time I thought ahead like you're always tellin' me."

He reached under the truck seat and pulled out a full bottle of whiskey. Les grinned in the darkness.

"Man, all we need is some of them French appetizers and we'd be high class."

Dirk punched him in the arm and took the first swig.

* * *

Monday, April 29th, 9 a.m.
Newport at the Marine Science Center

"Good morning," Kim said as Dr. Bolny came down the hall with his swinging stride.

He almost walked right past her before he realized she had spoken.

"Oh, hi Kim. Grim news. It's happened again. A mother and a baby washed ashore an hour ago at Eureka. I just got the call."

"Bullet holes?"

"The bodies are a mess — they've been pretty well ripped up by predators, but I did ask the researcher who called to probe around the skull. If they find anything, they'll call back."

Kim walked on to the library. Today, she was supposed to be working on a paper and needed to gather some background information. Jack was at a table in the back, taking notes from recent marine biology journals. He looked up as Kim came near.

"Hi? You don't look especially happy today either. Seems like I often catch you that way. What's wrong?"

"Two more grays are dead. Dr. Bolny just told me."

"Shot like the others?"

"He doesn't know yet, but I bet they were. Ohhhh, how can people be so evil?"

She pounded her fist on the table. Jack took her by the arm and walked her over to an alcove.

"Look, Kim. The first rule of a good researcher is not to get emotionally involved with your work. If you get upset about things, you can't analyze the facts rationally."

"Oh Jack, I don't buy that at all. How can you even be interested in something if you don't care? I think caring is what drives a good researcher."

"Kim, caring and being torn apart by your emotions are two different things."

He tried to take her arm, but Kim was in high gear. Cheeks flushed, she replied.

"Maybe you can do that — I can't. There has to be something I can do, and believe me if there is, I will."

Shaking his head, Jack watched her as she stormed off toward Dr. Bolny's office.

Dr. Bolny didn't seem surprised to see her. He was talking on the phone but gestured for her to sit down. When he hung up, he turned to her.

"Same thing. The mother's just too big to probe, but they found a bullet in the baby's skull — went right through his brain."

He turned to a map of the Pacific Ocean and put two more pins in it.

"Last winter, four whales were found — San Diego, two at Florence, and another at Seaside. Look, here are the dates they were found."

Kim went over to look at the map as Dr. Bolny pointed out dates and locations.

"Seaside December 19; Florence December 21; San Diego January 8. Now look here. The blue pins are for those whales found in December and January. The red ones are for the ones found this month. Notice the dates. What do you think?"

Kim gasped.

"They're in chronological order — like someone is going up and down the coast and killing them in order. The first group proceed from north to south and this group is south to north. If Eureka was the last, then...."

Dr. Bolny finished it for her.

"Whoever it is is headed this way."

Chapter 17

Foxhunts and Whale Parties

Monday, April 29th, 7:30 p.m.
Newport, Oregon

At the monthly meeting of the Lincoln County Amateur Radio Club, Kim stood as introductions were made. Gary, N6GP, had called her that afternoon to remind her of the meeting.

"I know you'll only be here for the term, but you might enjoy some of our activities. And the club would also be a good group to tell about the incidents with whales."

Kim was surprised to find so many guests at the meeting. Several out-of-town Amateur Radio operators visiting the scenic Oregon coast had seen the club meeting announced in the local paper and decided to drop by. Kim sat next to N7GSU, a former police officer and federal agent who was taking a brief coastal holiday before moving to Alaska. He listened intently as she told him about the mystery about the whales.

"Wish I were going to be around to help, but we're leaving in three days. That sounds like the kind of intrigue I'd like to solve. My wife and I are staying here in town at the Barracuda Motel — if anything comes up in the next couple of days and I can help, let me know."

The meeting began and after the business part, Kim was again introduced to the group by Gary. Quickly, she explained what had been happening to the gray whales.

"I don't know what I'm asking you to look for, but I know a number of you operate fishing boats, and Gary said someone in the club has a whale-watching charter service."

A couple in the back stood

"I'm John — N7YSQ and this is my wife, Helen."

"Hi," Kim said. "If you see anything unusual — such as someone getting too close to a gray whale, please contact the Coast Guard or the Marine Science Center."

"If you see anyone operating firearms from a boat, please let us know that too," added Gary.

"You bet," said John. "We'll be glad to help."

"What makes you think we'll see anything in this area?" Johnny James, N7YSQ, asked. "So far none of the dead whales has been here."

"We're not sure," said Kim. "That's why we've passed the information along on maritime nets to Amateur Radio operators all the way from Baja to the Arctic. But there does seem to be a geographic progression to the killings, and it appears that they're moving this way."

The group all offered to help. Then the discussion turned to a fund-raising project to buy radio equipment for the local high school. After the members broke for cookies and coffee, N7MBK, a longtime member of the club approached her.

"Kim, I'm in charge of a transmitter hunt we're having this Thursday night, and I was wondering if you'd like to be the 'fox.' This group all loves to 'hunt' and frankly, we're having trouble finding someone to be the hidden transmitter. Don't feel you have to — we understand if you're too busy with your studies."

Kim smiled.

"I'd love to! And I know the perfect place. You know I went on a few foxhunts in Salem when I was in high school and I always wished I could be the one to hide. Guess that goes back to my hide and seek days when I loved to find places where no one could find me."

"Great! Why don't you be here at 6:30 and we'll send you with someone. We usually have everyone work in pairs — both the hiders and the seekers."

Kim left the group with a warm sense of belonging. Thursday would be fun. Transmitter or "fox" or "bunny" hunts involved one person hiding with a transmitter. The "hunters" then using directional finders or just their two-meter antennas set out to search. The team with the lowest elapsed mileage from the starting point who located the hidden transmitter won.

Kim thought about where she would hide. Just north of Newport, there was a bluff overlooking a rocky beach. There were several stands of shore pine there. She didn't think she could get down to the beach, but she could hide behind the big boulders at the edge of the bluff.

She'd stopped there the Sunday she was whale watching at Rocky Creek. As she was driving back to the Marine Science Center after her unhappy meeting with Marc, she'd pulled her car on the turnout to sit and think a minute. The sight of three more migrating gray whales had cheered her momentarily, and she'd thought at the time that it was a perfect place to watch the horizon.

Gary told her good-bye and promised that he'd let them know at the Marine Science Center if there were any developments.

The girls were making popcorn in her apartment when she returned.

"Have fun?" Julia asked.

"Yeah, I volunteered to go on a foxhunt."

"Foxhunt? I thought you were against hunting?"

Kim laughed and sat down to explain.

* * *

Tuesday, April 30th, midnight
Interstate 5 north of Portland

As usual after a drug pickup from the cave, George preferred to get on the road immediately. There was less traffic at night and as long as he was careful to keep under the speed limit, he felt little fear of being stopped. Les and Dirk slept, leaning on each other in the small confines of the truck cab.

The delivery tonight was for Seattle. Usually the drugs that went there came from bigger sources, but someone named John had called saying he needed ten kilos. George was happy to get rid of it in large quantities. The fewer deliveries he had to make the better.

Actually, there was no reason for Dirk and Les to come along, but they had an unwritten agreement that they all went together on everything. Perhaps it was lack of trust or perhaps it was just habit, but that was the way they started the operation and that was the way they were continuing it.

George rubbed his left arm gingerly. Coming out of the cave tonight, a wave had smashed him into a rock. The jagged rock edge had sliced through his wetsuit and cut his upper arm. Now bandaged under his shirt, he hoped it wouldn't get infected or stiff. They would probably have many more pickups in the next two weeks and he needed to be in good condition.

They should reach Seattle around 5 a.m.. There was the possibility of another call coming in as early as tonight so there would be no leisure time. Once the drugs were out of the truck, he would let Dirk or Les drive home. He never really slept when one of them was at the wheel, but maybe he could doze.

He turned on the windshield wipers as rain started falling. He was glad the storm had waited until after they had done the cave pickup — it was rough going even in good weather. Who knew what it would be like later in the week?

* * *

Wednesday May 1st, 8 a.m.
Gold Beach, Oregon

Myrna and Howard Lindstrom had been up for hours. Early morning was their favorite time of day. They loved walking the beaches in front of their condominium with their Golden Retriever, Maxine. They also loved watching for whales. Last weekend, they had hosted their annual "Whale of a Party" at which fifty friends and neighbors joined them for an afternoon of wine, hors d'oeuvres, and fun.

A highlight of the day had been Howard's slide show of their trip to Baja in March. They had gone out on Scammon's Lagoon in a lightweight skiff and actually petted the gray whales that came up to them. Myrna still bubbled enthusiastically when she talked about mother whales shoving their babies up to be petted by humans.

"They loved to be touched just as much as you do, Maxine," Myrna told their dog who was running in circles around them as they walked down the beach.

The dog brought a stick and dropped it at Howard's feet. He obligingly picked it up and threw it.

"I imagine most of the whales are north of here now, dear. Next year, maybe we'll have the party a week earlier. It would be fun for everyone if we saw more of them."

The group had spotted three during the four-hour party, but no one watched consistently. Howard and Myrna walked along arm in arm, reminiscing. Sunlight peeked through clouds and warmed the brisk wind. They'd heard a storm system had moved into the northern part of the state, but so far there had been no rain in Gold Beach. As they reached the end of their usual walking distance and started to turn around, Myrna caught her husband's arm.

"Look dear!" she said, pointing out to sea. "Do you see one blowing?"

Howard pulled out the pair of binoculars he always carried in his jacket and raised them to his eyes.

"Yes, yes I do. And it's not just one — it's two. Looks like a big one and a little one. Here, look."

She took the field glasses and stared intently out to sea.

"A mother and a baby — just a little slower than the rest. Well, the dear things. I hope they're getting along okay."

* * *

Wednesday, May 1st, noon
Newport

Kim, Julia and Chris were concocting a different kind of whale party. Sunday was Dr. Bolny's 50th birthday and other than the fact that the date coincided with Cinco de Mayo, no one had thought of anything clever. During their lunch break, Kim told them a little of what she had been thinking.

"I wish we could do something with Bertha — like have the whale's head say happy birthday. My Uncle Steve sent me a gadget last week that he bought at a swap meet. I mentioned to him that I wanted to do something remote control and he sent me this."

Kim opened a drawer and pulled out a small gray box.

"It's called a Dual Tone Multi Function decoder."

"Sorry, Kim, but you're going to have to speak English."

"Remember how I showed you that I could light up an unattached light bulb by just aiming the antenna of my handheld at it and depressing the push to talk button?"

"Yeah, that was neat."

"Well, this device — connected to my old two-meter rig — allows up to nine functions. Each number on my touchtone key pad can activate a different one. See," she said, pulling her second transceiver, a small pocket-sized state of the art model from her pocket.

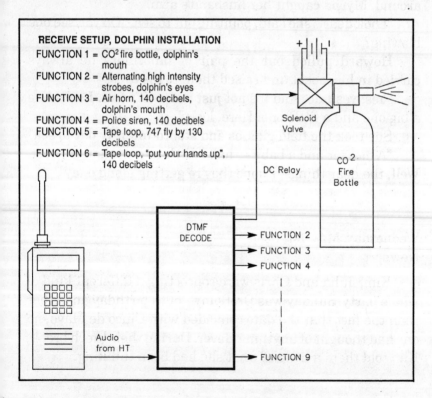

RECEIVE SETUP, DOLPHIN INSTALLATION

FUNCTION 1 = CO_2 fire bottle, dolphin's mouth
FUNCTION 2 = Alternating high intensity strobes, dolphin's eyes
FUNCTION 3 = Air horn, 140 decibels, dolphin's mouth
FUNCTION 4 = Police siren, 140 decibels
FUNCTION 5 = Tape loop, 747 fly by 130 decibels
FUNCTION 6 = Tape loop, "put your hands up", 140 decibels

Solenoid Valve

DC Relay

CO_2 Fire Bottle

DTMF DECODE

FUNCTION 2
FUNCTION 3
FUNCTION 4

FUNCTION 9

Audio from HT

"For instance, when I touch number one, it could trigger a tape loop that would say 'Happy Birthday.' But I haven't gone beyond that. Any ideas?"

"How about red lights for the eyes?" Chris suggested.

"I've got an old car alarm that I found so annoying I disconnected," Julia said. "It's up in the apartment in my closet."

The three of them made a list, laughing at some of the suggestions. By the end of the hour, they had a pile of possible special effects including an outdated fire extinguisher Kim had found.

"You think this thing still works?" Chris asked.

"I don't know, but if we use it, that's it. I don't want to spend money to get the thing recharged. I guess that will be the great effect. Uncle Steve sent me a solenoid valve and several DC relays — you know, I'm not really sure how all this stuff fits together, but I have a schedule with him tonight, and I'll ask."

The three birthday conspirators secreted their surprise ingredients away and went back to the assigned lab tasks. At the end of the afternoon, Kim promised them if she couldn't get her radio idea working, they would think of something else. She walked back to the apartment with Julia.

The savory smell of spaghetti greeted them as they opened the apartment door. Megan was hard at work in the kitchen.

"Twenty minutes to dinner, you two. Thought I'd make it Italian night."

"Smells wonderful," Kim said. "You're an angel come to rescue us from our own cooking."

Ten minutes to six. She would have just enough time for her schedule with Uncle Steve before dinner. Hurriedly, she washed up and sat down at her low-band transceiver.

"W6RHM from KA7SJP."

She called him on schedule on twenty meters, knowing that if he had gotten away from work on time, that he was now homeward-bound on the L.A. freeways. He had installed the low-band rig in his car just last year, and Kim was delighted to be able to talk to him almost every day.

"KA7SJP from W6RHM. Good evening, Kim. I'm out here on the 405 with 10,000 of my best friends."

There was a loud honk in the background and the squealing of tires.

"Are you okay, Uncle Steve?"

"Oh sure — just the usual evening camaraderie among commuters. What's up?"

Quickly, she explained the party idea they were planning for Dr. Bolny.

"Like I told you when you sent that decoder. I think I understand how that works but I'm not sure how to hook up everything."

"What all have you got?"

She told him the list of possibles.

"Tell you what, Kim, why don't I send you a fax of the diagram to get it all going. Do you have a fax number where your birthday guest won't see it?"

"Well, I guess maybe to Florence Bund's office. Just a minute while I look it up."

They chatted a few minutes more and then Kim thanked him and signed. The spaghetti was ready.

Chapter 18

What the Fox Saw

Thursday, May 2nd, 7 p.m.
Newport, Oregon

T rue to his word, Uncle Steve sent a fax showing detailed instructions how to hook up all the special devices Kim wanted the whale's head to perform. Kim alerted Florence Bund not to tell Dr. Bolny.

"Having a surprise party, are you? That's great. I love surprises. Can I help?"

"Just help us think of a way to get Dr. Bolny here Sunday evening. Since he's returning home from that symposium Saturday night, he probably wouldn't be planning on coming down here Sunday. How do you think we can lure him to the center?"

"Why don't we ask his wife to help. She could pretend to be taking him out to dinner or something."

"Great idea, Florence."

"Good. I'll talk to her today — glad to be part of the party planning. By the way, just what are you all up to anyway? That diagram looks pretty complicated."

"Just something fun — don't worry."

The thought of the surprise kept Kim's imagination working all day as she went about her studies. She had decided on six things that ol' Bertha could do. But she probably wouldn't have time to hook any of them up until tomorrow.

There was an international Marine Science Symposium in Portland Friday and Saturday, and practically all the students and staff were planning on going. Kim thought she might drive up Saturday to sit in on some of the sessions, but she really needed to catch up on her school projects tomorrow. She would just have to wait and see if she had time.

"And here I am going to sit out on a bluff and play Amateur Radio games tonight," she scolded herself as she drove up the coast highway to the fairgrounds where the club met. "Priorities, priorities! This is important," she said, already feeling a shiver of excitement about getting to hide with the transmitter.

Ron, the club president was just opening up the club meeting room when she arrived. While they waited for Jeri Smither, her foxhunt partner, Ron told Kim about his fascination with finding hidden transmitters.

"Actually it started out of self-defense. About ten years ago, there was terrible television interference on one of our channels. I talked to neighbors and they were all experiencing it. Then I heard that since I had an antenna tower in my yard, everyone suspected that I was the one causing the problem. You know, ham radio operators are always the suspects, and they're usually not the culprits."

"I even contacted the FCC to verify that my own equipment was clean. An engineer there suggested that I look for a television booster amplifier that was self-oscillating and radiating through someone's television antenna. So with the help of a friend, I hooked my two-meter beam to a five-inch TV and put it in the car. We then began a sweep of the neighborhood.

"We finally pinned it down to a couple of houses — asked the residents one by one to turn off their sets. The third house was the one. When they turned off theirs, the interference went away. We helped them get a replacement of the faulty part. They were really grateful and embarrassed — admitted that they thought, just like everybody else in the neighborhood, that it was my fault! I felt like putting a big sign in the front yard that said 'I am innocent!' "

Kim laughed. They shared stories for fifteen more minutes. Then someone called Ron on the local repeater. It was a friend of Jeri's explaining that Jeri had an emergency and wouldn't be able to make it.

"Well let's just wait for the others to get here, and I'll send someone else out with you."

"No, I'd like to go now before they start arriving. Don't worry about me. I'll be fine. I'm afraid you're going to find me before it's really dark anyway."

Ron protested, but Kim insisted. She gathered up the transmitter that was to be the fox and put it in her car. The two-meter transmitter would emit a continuous tone on a simplex frequency. The "hunters" using various antennas — everything from loops to handheld three-element beams — would zero in on the place where the signal strength was the greatest. Then the search would be intensified until Kim and the transmitter were found.

Happily, she drove to the bluff she had spotted just north of Newport. Making sure that no cars were coming, she pulled her car onto a side road on the east side of the highway and hid it under some trees. It was probable that some of the hams might be driving down the highway right now on their way to the club meeting place. If they saw her standing there, the hunt would be over before it started.

She waited under a tree until she was sure the road was clear and then dashed across the highway, carrying her gear.

There was a grassy path to the rock outcropping that hung over the ocean's edge. Kim placed the "fox" transmitter behind one rock and turned it on. Then she picked up her own two-meter rig and keyed up the local repeater frequency to tell Ron that the fox was now in place and that the hunt could begin.

She settled down on the cool ground, her back to a boulder, where she could see the road without being seen. On her handheld, she listened in on some of the chatter between teams. There was some good natured banter about being close to the find. She saw several cars with antennas go by, but no one stopped. Then one car slowed. There was no place to park on the side where Kim was. The car continued on down the road and turned around on the side road where her car was hidden. Slowly, it came back again but continued on past her.

She giggled as she saw headlights turn onto the side road and stop. Somebody had figured out that this was the closest place to park to where she was. Now if they could find her on foot. She instinctively scrunched down behind the rock, feeling the same excitement she used to as a kid playing hide and seek.

Now she could hear footsteps scrunching through the gravel on the edge of the road. She wanted to peek but was afraid of giving away her position. She guessed it was just one person because there was no conversation. Odd. Ron had said everyone went out in teams. The footsteps were on the other side of the rock. She was just debating whether she should stand up and "surrender" when a familiar voice said, "Kim?"

"Marc!"

She scrambled up almost knocking over the hidden transmitter.

"What are you doing here?"

"I was just driving over to see if I could visit you when I heard the local hams on the repeater and gathered that a foxhunt was already underway. Someone mentioned your name so I decided to join in. Hope you don't mind...."

"Of course not," Kim said coming out to stand beside him. "By the way, congratulations on finding me. How did you know I'd be on this side of the road?"

"Well, that's what my signal-strength meter was indicating, plus I just knew that if you had your choice, you'd pick a spot with an ocean view."

Kim laughed. This was the old Marc she knew — the one who teased her and was fun to be with. Just then, three other hams arrived, carrying antennas. They stopped when they saw Marc.

"Darn! I was sure we'd be first."

"You are," Marc said handing them the fox transmitter. "I had an unfair advantage. I knew the quarry and her method of operation. Besides, I'm not a member of the club and I didn't register for this."

"Are you sure?"

"Absolutely, I just came to visit Kim."

The men took the transmitter and invited Kim and Marc to come back to the club with them for refreshments and the presentation of the prize: a coffee cup with a fox on it.

Kim thanked them but explained that she really needed to get back to study plus she wanted to visit with Marc a little.

She smiled as they walked away carrying their "fox" and reporting back to Ron that the prey had been found.

Marc and Kim stood silently after the men left. Awkwardly, Kim turned to Marc.

"It's a beautiful night, isn't it?"

"It is," he agreed.

The moon had come up and was casting slivers of white over the dark waters. A wave dashed up against the rock cliff sending a spray of silver foam high in the air.

"Kim, I'm sorry."

"Sorry about what?"

"Sorry, I wrecked what has been the best friendship of my life. Can we just go back to the way we were and let the future take care of itself?"

"I'd like that Marc. I'd like that very much."

She turned to him and then he was kissing her, and she was kissing him back. She felt like laughing and crying all at the same time. Hand in hand, they walked toward the bluff and sat down on the rocks, looking out at the moonlit sea.

The events of the past weeks came out in a rush as they both told each other of their activities of the past weeks. Several times they interrupted each other and then laughed. This was what had been so wonderful about their friendship — the sharing of all that they did.

Marc seemed keenly interested in the mystery surrounding the deaths of the gray whales.

"Any leads?"

"Not yet. Just waiting for someone to see something and report it. It's bound to happen sooner or later."

"What was that?" Marc whispered.

"What was what?"

"Voices. I heard voices over the edge."

"Impossible — it's too rough for anyone to get down there."

The two of them walked over to the edge and leaned over the side. Kim turned to Marc and put her finger to her lips. Far below them bouncing through the rough surf was a rubber boat with three men in wetsuits in it. It looked like they were coming out from underneath the very bluff that Kim and Marc stood on. The waves slammed them into the rocks and one of the men swore loudly as he reached out with a paddle and pushed away from the cliff.

Fascinated, Kim and Marc watched as the men battled their way out through the surf. Just then one of the men looked up and pointed. Instinctively, Kim and Marc dropped to their knees behind the rocks.

"Who are they?" Marc whispered.

"I don't know," Kim whispered back and then giggled. "I don't know why we're whispering. They can't hear us over the surf."

"We heard them."

"Yeah, but they must have been right under us."

Kim pointed to a crevice in the rocks.

"Their voices must have been coming up through here."

"What on Earth would someone be doing down there?"

"I don't know, but it sure seems like a strange place to be taking a boat ride."

* * *

"Did they see us?"

"I'm sure of it. Didn't you see how they ducked out of sight?" Les asked.

They were back to the beach now and hauling the boat and their cocaine bundles up the embankment.

"So what? — some people standing out watching the moonlight and they see some guys in a boat. No way they could know what we're doing."

"Only one thing bothers me," said George.

"What's that?"

"I recognized one of them. When she turned her head, I saw it was our friend from the other night — you know, 'Little Miss Ponytail.'"

"Oh well — big deal. Come on. Let's get on the road. I didn't want to make this pickup so early in the night, but it'll take us until morning to get to Yakima."

* * *

Kim and Marc sat drinking hot chocolate in the student lounge. Chris from the bone lab had joined them and he and Kim were telling Marc about the surprise they had cooked up for Dr. Bolny.

"Are you going back to OSU tonight?" Kim asked.

"I was planning on it, although my lab for tomorrow has been cancelled."

"You're welcome to stay with me," Chris offered. "I'm not going up to the symposium until Saturday morning."

Chris looked at Kim tentatively, trying to make sure she wanted her friend to stay. Kim spoke up enthusiastically.

"That's a great idea. Then maybe you can help us rig up the whale's head in the morning. We're having a few problems making everything work."

They talked awhile and then Chris left.

"Second apartment on the left — door's unlocked. You can use the bed in the front bedroom. Just make yourself at home."

Kim and Marc walked down the hallway together, Kim pointing out the various exhibits.

"I notice you didn't tell Chris what we saw tonight," Marc said.

"I'm not sure what we did see, are you? Who knows? A friend of mine at the Coast Guard said they get all kinds of crazy calls. Maybe it was college kids up to a prank or maybe it was...maybe it was someone hiding something," she finished softly.

"That's just what I was thinking, but thinking slowly to be honest. This has been a pretty long day. Why don't we talk about it in the morning?"

"Agreed. Breakfast at six? I'll even bake cinnamon rolls for you."

"At six? You haven't changed, have you, Kim? Normally, I'd sleep in until some decadent hour like seven or eight," Marc laughed. "But for cinnamon rolls..."

"I'm in apartment six. It's right around the corner from Chris's."

They walked down the corridor hand in hand.

"You're sure you don't mind my staying over, Kim?"

"No, I'm glad you are. I've missed you."

"Missing doesn't even come close to describing it."

Marc held her tight for a minute and then kissed her gently.

"Say goodnight to me in ten minutes?" Kim asked tapping her two-meter rig. "I've missed that too."

"You can count on it."

Chapter 19

The Cave

Friday, May 3rd, 8 a.m.
Newport Bay

"That was a great breakfast, Kim. I had forgotten what a good cook you are. I still tell people about that apple pie you made in an ice cube tray in the fire lookout."

Kim laughed. What a relief it was to have her easy friendly relationship back with Marc. As they walked down the road toward the highway, she couldn't imagine being happier.

"So, are you sorry you didn't go to Portland with the others?" he asked.

"No, I hadn't planned to go today anyway — maybe tomorrow. I'll just have to see."

"Well, I definitely have to get back to Corvallis tonight. I've promised to help repair the repeater on Mary's Peak tomorrow."

"Now who's the one who is too busy?" Kim teased.

"Okay, okay, turning the page as someone on the radio says. What do you think those guys were up to last night?"

"That's why we're walking down this road — there's a scuba instructor — also a ham — who might be able to tell us something. He lives just over there. Let's ask him what he knows about that part of the coastline. I don't know — maybe they were illegally harvesting sea urchins or something."

"There's always a purpose to everything you do, Kim. Even a stroll in the morning sunshine."

Kim glanced at Marc to see if he was being sarcastic, but his smile and a quick hug reassured her it was a compliment.

Arm in arm, they proceeded to the mobile home where Bill Edwards, Amateur Radio operator KA7MDM and scuba instructor, lived. He was sitting on his front porch sipping a cup of coffee and reading the morning paper. Kim introduced Marc and explained what she wanted to find out.

"I was exactly here," she said, pointing to a spot on a map he spread out on the table. "I know the rocks overhang there and I couldn't see what was below, but I just assumed it's more rocks. Any idea why someone would take a rubber boat in there?"

"There's a cave, if you're talking about the place I think you are, Kim. Pretty good size too, but it's rough getting in and out. I've helped the sheriff's department and Coast Guard a couple of times when we've had missing persons. If a body washed in there, it's possible it could get hung up on one of the rocky ledges. I've been on two searches — happily, I never found anyone."

"The men were in wetsuits," Kim said.

"Oh yeah — like I said. It's rough going in and out. You'd have to get out of the boat and kind of swim in. And, of course, you always need a wetsuit in Oregon water. As far as what they were up to, I don't know, but I can assure you, it wasn't sea urchins. Nobody would take that kind of risk to get urchins even as valuable as they are."

"Any way we could get into that cave and take a look ourselves?" Marc asked.

"You a diver?"

"Naui certified."

"How about you?"

"I'm afraid not," Kim said. "That's one hobby I haven't had time to look into. But I'd sure like to help."

"You can. I admit that you've got my curiosity up now too. I've got some things I have to do this morning, but if you come back at one, I'll take you up there — even loan you a wetsuit. But let's get one thing clear — I'm not responsible for your safety. I'm taking you at your word that you're competent in the water."

"I understand," said Marc.

The two of them walked back to the Marine Science Center. Marc was obviously excited at the prospect of the adventure.

"You don't suppose I could learn to dive in three hours, do you?" Kim asked laughing.

"Not a chance. Boy, this is a switch. Usually, you're the one off doing stuff and I'm left behind. But seriously, Kim, you won't be left behind. Let's rig up a waterproof covering for my two-meter rig so I can tell you immediately what's in the cave. You may need to call the Coast Guard."

"Really? What do you think is in there?"

"Drugs," said Marc.

They walked across the parking lot in silence, but as they entered the lobby of the Marine Science Center, Kim turned to Marc.

"I know your mind is on this afternoon, Marc, and I'm wondering what we're getting into. But since we have a couple of hours free, do you think you could help Chris and me rig up that whale's head?"

"Sure, let's do it."

Chris was already down in the bone lab compiling some data for a research paper.

"Hey, you two. I thought you'd disappeared. You were gone before I woke up, Marc."

"Kim's an early riser and an early chef," said Marc. "And we just got back from a walk."

Kim looked at him, wondering if he was going to tell Chris about what they had planned for the afternoon. He didn't. Instead, he started looking at the setup Kim and Chris had already put in place inside Bertha's head.

Kim explained what they had so far.

"Number one on my key pad will actuate the DC relay that in turn actuates the solenoid valve on top of this fire extinguisher. We don't know if the fire extinguisher is still good, so we're taking a chance on that one. My uncle sent me a drawing of how to hook it up."

"Looks good. And what's this?"

"I'll show you."

Kim pushed number two on her two-meter key pad and a small tape recorder inside Bertha started rolling. Marc laughed as a deep male voice boomed out.

"This is the voice of ghost whales. I speak to you from the great beyond. Come closer so I can give you my secret message."

"Kind of morbid for a birthday party, don't you think, Kim?"

"Hold on. Here's where I need your help. There's a twenty-second pause on the tape where I assume Dr. Bolny will be moving closer. Then the message continues. Listen."

A chorus of cheerful voices broke into "Happy Birthday to you!"

"But when Dr. Bolny moves up to the whale's head, we want a container of confetti to open from the ceiling and shower down on him. How are we going to do that?"

"With one of your relays and some sort of container that either opens or tips. I think a pulley that tips it will be easiest. What else do you have?"

"Red strobe lights that flash for the eyes. Here, let me show you. They look really eerie when the lights are turned off. Problem is, they haven't been working every time."

They worked that time and Marc whistled in admiration. When Chris flipped the room lights back on, Marc bent over the wiring looking for a short.

"And we've got this car alarm too — you know, one of those obnoxious ones that just goes on and on. I haven't hooked it up yet, but I'd like it to be number five — the last thing we do because it's so noisy. Then after that, everyone who has been hiding down the hall will come pouring into the room and we'll escort Dr. Bolny back down to the student lounge where the cake and other refreshments will be set up."

"You're going to a lot of trouble to surprise this guy — he must be a pretty special instructor."

"He is," Kim and Chris said in unison.

* * *

"I can hardly wait for Sunday night. Thanks a lot for helping," Kim told Marc as they drove down to pick up Bill at his home.

"My pleasure — just wish I could be here to see it all in action."

"Sure you don't want to stay the rest of the weekend?"

"I wish I could, but no. I've got to go back."

They stopped in front of Bill's place and went up on the porch. Bill had Marc try on a wetsuit he had for him. It fit perfectly.

"Come on you two — let's go in my truck. I've got the boat loaded in the back."

As they walked outside to climb in the weatherbeaten Dodge, something clicked in Kim's brain.

"What is it, Kim? What are you doing?"

She was standing at the back of the truck, looking at a half-deflated rubber Zodiac that was folded over in the truck bed.

"It's like the one the men had the other night," she said.

"What is?"

"The boat."

Bill laughed.

"If you think I spend my evenings out running around in caves battling the surf, you overestimate my ambition, Kim."

"Oh no, Bill. I didn't mean you. I mean I think I know where I've seen them and that boat before. I think maybe it was those same creeps that chased me home one night."

"What Kim? I never heard about this."

"No, I never told you. I've seen them twice. Once when I was alone and once when I went out to dinner with a friend. They drive an old blue pickup with a boat in the back."

"Lots of folks around here have rubber boats."

"I know that Bill. Maybe I'm wrong but I have a hunch they were the same guys."

They drove up the highway and Kim pointed out the exact spot where she and Marc were when they saw the men.

"Yeah, this is where I thought it was. The cave is right under this overhang. There's a beach less than a half mile south of here where we can get in."

Bill turned the truck around and drove back the way they came. At a wide spot in the road, he pulled over.

"It's a pretty rough trail down, but Marc and I can make it fine. We'll put in here and run up to the cave. If we find something, Marc can radio you. If there are drugs in that cave, I want the Coast Guard here when we bring them ashore."

"Okay, I'll monitor for you on simplex."

She watched the two of them load the boat, now inflated, on their shoulders and start the trek down the slippery rock surface. Marc had made a quick waterproof pack for his two-meter rig out of neoprene, and it was lashed securely to the inside of the boat.

Kim settled down in the truck to wait. Bill had left the keys behind for her "just in case." She didn't ask him what he meant by that. If the three guys showed up, it would be up to her to call for help, alert Marc and Bill, and scoot out of there as fast as possible. She looked at her watch. 2:15.

There was light traffic on the highway. With fair weather forecast for the weekend, Kim imagined that by late afternoon, people would begin flocking in. She watched every car that went by, but none turned. It was 2:30.

"KA7ITR from KA7SJP."

No answer. They must be busy navigating the boat. In fact, she doubted if Marc would hear her unless he put the transceiver right up to his ear. 2:45. Suppose something happened to them? What kind of a crazy thing were they doing anyway? Would Marc have gone ahead with this if she had spoken out against it? Three o'clock. Where were they?

She wished she'd asked him to transmit when they had reached the cave. She guessed that he wouldn't bother until he was safely back outside. How would she know if they got into trouble? 3:10.

Kim twisted her hands nervously. She got out of the truck and stood on the edge of the bluff looking northward. There was a large stand of windswept trees that effectively blocked her view of the coastline where it jogged eastward from where she stood. 3:20. Maybe she should drive up to the bluff where the transmitter hunt had been and see if she could see them from there.

"KA7SJP from KA7ITR."

"Marc — are you okay?"

He sounded breathless and she could hear waves crashing against rocks.

"Fine. Call the Coast Guard and call the Newport Police. Direct them to your location."

"Then you found something?"

"And then some. We'll be there shortly."

Quickly, Kim punched up the local repeater. Perhaps Gary would be on duty and monitoring. Otherwise, she would call 911.

"N6GP from KA7SJP."

"Hi Kim. KA7SJP from N6GP. What's up?"

"Are you at the station?"

"No, in my car on my way there now. I took a late lunch. Just heading back."

"Gary, I can't explain much on the air, but we've found something. Can you send someone down to meet us and can you notify the Newport Police too. Remember where I hid the transmitter the other night? I'm just about one half mile south of that on the west side of the road. Sitting in a brown Dodge pickup."

"I'll be right there, Kim. Are you sure you're okay?"

"Absolutely. I think you'll be very interested in what we've found."

Chapter 20

Evil Heading South;
Whales Swimming North

Friday, May 3rd, 4 p.m.
Just south of Yakima

"Quit your grumbling! I'm sick of hearing you complain," George shouted at Les.

"You said we were going to have two days off. Me and Dirk was gonna have some fun. Now we're back on the same road we just got off."

"I can't believe you'd complain about a customer who decides he needs to double his order on the spot. Don't you realize how much more of the stuff that means will be gone? We're that much closer to being paid on this shipment and we're getting paid tomorrow on the last. You guys ought to be happy."

"Why couldn't he have told us before we left the coast? I mean it's not like this place is exactly next door to us," Dirk persisted.

"Yeah, or why don't we just carry extra along on all our deliveries just in case?" Les asked.

"Do you know what would happen to us if we were ever stopped and searched and the cops found drugs on board? Do you guys ever think about that when we're driving to deliver. In fact, do you ever think?"

The men were silent as George continued.

"That's why I do the driving. I don't like Dirk's lead foot on the pedal or Les's habit of passing everyone on the road. I'm always relieved when the truck is empty. At least that way, we're only at risk one way."

Les and Dirk began to grow restless listening to their boss's lengthy explanation.

"So what if we have to go back and pick up some more tonight? Like I told you, the *Si Maria* is supposed to dock early tomorrow morning. I'm going to meet with Freddie at 10 a.m. and get paid, and when I get paid, you guys get paid."

"Yeah, you're going all alone as usual. How do we even know if...?"

"Go ahead and finish that sentence, Les."

"Naw. Forget it."

"I'll finish it for you. How do you know if I give you guys your equal share? Right?"

Les and Dirk were silent.

"Well, I guess you don't. But I'm not taking you with me. And you ask why not — I'll tell you why not. This guy Freddie is really nervous. He didn't like it when he heard I had hired you two to help me. The way he figures it the less people who know about the drugs, the better. I guess he's gotten used to the idea now, but I'm afraid if he actually met you, he'd start worrying."

"Worrying about what?" Dirk growled.

"About whether you'd talk to the wrong people."

"Do we strike you as snitches?"

"No. Let's just say, I think you'd make him nervous."

Les and Dirk sat digesting this latest conversation. What George didn't tell them was that he thought Freddie would think they were stupid. And stupid people scared Freddie.

"So you don't get to go with me," continued George. "I'll be back at the motel by eleven and divide the money. If that's not good enough for you, then I guess we shouldn't be doing business together."

There was no comment. Without George to arrange things, there would have been no money to begin with. Still, they didn't like the arrangement and it showed on their sullen faces. Even after George turned on a country western station, they were silent.

"No singalongs?" questioned George. "What's wrong with you cowpokes anyway?"

Gradually the mood eased, and by the time they were to Portland, Dirk was talking about how they would spend their next payoff.

* * *

Friday, May 3rd, 5 p.m.
Newport, Oregon

It was nearly five before Kim and Marc finished telling both the Coast Guard and the Newport Police how they had happened to find the bundles of cocaine.

"Thirty-six kilos here," Captain John Stills of the Newport Police said, whistling under his breath. "Quite a haul. This represents a lot of money that's not going to be made by some pretty vicious people, and it probably represents quite a few lives saved because the stuff's not going out into the public."

"You're sure no one saw you going into the cave?"

"We sure didn't see anyone, and Kim stood guard down the road at the beach. Nobody stopped or even slowed while she was there," Marc said.

"You said you might have seen these men before?" the captain asked, turning to Kim.

"Yeah, maybe a couple of times, but I'm not sure. There was a night several weeks ago when I was in Old Town and three drunks came out of the Pelican Bar. They kind of hassled me and even chased me in their truck, but that was all there was to it."

The captain seemed concerned.

"Do they know you?"

"No. I may have seen them drive by one other time, but on both occasions it was so dark, I couldn't tell you what they looked like."

"Then why do you think it's the same guys?"

"The boat for one thing — they had a Zodiac in their pickup, and just something about the profile of the one fellow looked familiar. But like I said. I'm not sure. I couldn't pick them out of a lineup or anything."

"Well, we'll ask some questions around. In the meantime, this is the end of your involvement in this. Do you understand?" he asked looking at Kim and Marc directly. "Yes," they both said in unison.

The captain continued to stare at them as if worried about what schemes they might have. Then he turned to the investigator from the Coast Guard to make plans for surveillance of the area. Members of the Drug Enforcement Agency in Portland would be here in the morning. Until then, the Coast Guard would make frequent patrols of the shore line in both directions and police would monitor the highway.

Bill Edwards stayed behind to answer a few more questions. Gary from the Coast Guard who had also come to the scene offered to drive Kim and Marc back to the Marine Science Center.

"You heard what the police captain said, didn't you?" he said to Kim.

"Yes. Oh don't tell me, you're going to lecture me too."

"Seriously, Kim. The time to have called us was before you set out to go in the cave. I'm just happy nothing happened to any of you. What would your parents think if they knew about this?"

"They'd have a cow," said Kim softly.

Gary dropped them off at the foot of the access road as he needed to get back to the station. Kim and Marc were silent as they walked back to the center.

Suddenly, Marc burst out laughing.

"What's so funny?"

"I can't believe it. Here I am away from you for almost a month and my life is dreadfully calm, in fact, almost boring. Now I've been with you for less than 24 hours and you've got me involved in apprehending drug dealers, worrying about dead whales, and wiring a skull to frighten a professor."

"Sorry you came?"

"No, I'm happier than I've been in a long time. Most of all, I'm happy to be with you."

* * *

Friday, May 3rd, 5 p.m.
Longview, Washington

In contrast to Marc's ebullient mood, Freddie's was sour. As they approached the Oregon-Washington border, he stood up from his navigator's desk and walked outside on the deck. Heavy cloud cover stretched as far as he could see. It had been that way for days. Clouds that rolled in at night and then cleared for partial sunshine during the day.

There had been no hunting in over a week. They were due into Newport tonight — would probably be there at least a day and a half to unload some lumber that was being transferred down from Vancouver. Somehow, even the thought of meeting George set his already frayed nerves even further on edge.

Sure, George pretended to be his buddy — always greeted him like a long lost friend. But that was because Freddie came bearing the payoff money. He had no illusions that George really liked him. That was the way it was with everyone. They were only nice to him if they were getting something out of him.

He felt anger course up his spine, stiffening the hair at the back of his neck. He needed a release. They would soon be out of whale country as most of the grays were already north of them. He went back to his table and scanned the weather reports that had just come in. Clear skies were predicted for tomorrow and the next day.

Maybe — maybe if they got underway on schedule, conditions would be right for a little hunting on their way to the Oregon-California border. He held that thought as solace as night approached.

* * *

Friday May 3rd, 7 p.m
Newport, Oregon

"KA7SJP from KG7FS."
"Go ahead KG7FS."

"Hi Kim. My name is Mike Miller — I heard you passing information along to the maritime net the other morning, and I just wanted to offer my help too. I live on my boat here in Astoria and have pretty good contact with the locals who operate commercial fishing boats. Anything specifically I can do to help?"

"That's great Mike. Just pass the word along to everyone to keep their eyes out for anyone shooting a rifle from a boat."

"I'll do that, Kim."

They chatted a minute and then signed. Kim was tempted to stay on the air and work some DX (distance) but she had schoolwork to catch up on. Marc had left for Corvallis just an hour ago, promising that they would keep the 10 p.m. two-meter schedule they'd had now for almost two years.

While she was making herself a bowl of soup and a sandwich, Kim turned on the rig. That was when she'd heard Mike's CQ. An unanswered CQ to her was as irresistible as a ringing phone. She was glad she'd gone back to him, but now it was time to hit her books and get busy on a report that was due.

"Hey, Kim."

Chris was standing in the open doorway.

"Hi."

"Marc told me about your adventures this afternoon on his way out. How'd you two manage to keep your plans quiet this morning when we were working on the skull?"

He sounded a little hurt, as though they had purposefully been hiding something from him.

"Chris, I really didn't know what we were getting into. I guess Marc suspected there would be drugs all along, but I don't think I believed it until I saw them pull up in the boat. Even now, it seems unreal."

"Okay — but next time you go out on a high seas adventure, invite me along."

"Okay, Chris, I will. But I hope there won't be any more adventures like that," Kim said laughing.

"What I really stopped by for was to ask if you wanted a ride up to Portland. I'm going first thing in the morning."

"You know, I guess not. I blew today. Now I have to catch up. And I want to make sure that whale head is functioning perfectly for the party. Promise me, you'll take good notes."

"Will do. Sorry to miss your company though."

After he left, Kim turned her attention back to her books, but it was hard to concentrate. She kept having visions of the three men in the truck who had chased her. Who were they?"

* * *

Captain John Stills was asking exactly the same question of the bartender at the Pelican Bar.

"Three guys — drive a pickup with a boat in the back."

"Lots of people have runabouts they haul around with them," said the bartender, "but there are three fellows who come around here occasionally. Maybe once every couple of weeks. I always kind of hate to see them come in because they usually get drunk. Once I even told them I wouldn't serve them anymore, and they didn't take to that kindly."

"Have any idea who they are?"

"Well one of them's named Les, I think. And Les and this other guy call the third one Boss. He seems to be the one who drinks the least — often tells them when it's time to leave and stuff."

"Do they live around here?"

"I haven't the faintest idea. Once I heard one of them say something about time to get on the road, but that could mean any road, I guess."

"Could you ask around and see if anyone knows them?"

"Sure, Captain. I'd be happy to help. What did these guys do anyway?"

"We're not sure they did anything. Just need to talk to them."

The captain gave him his card and left.

* * *

Friday, May 3rd, 11 p.m.
100 miles south of Newport

His mother was swimming more slowly fighting the strong current. Silver Star stayed close to her. She paused while he nursed and then resumed her tireless motion. It seemed like they had been swimming forever. His birth memories were fast fading. Life had always been this: swimming, nursing, and surfacing to breathe.

At night, the sea seemed even more alive than in the day. Without the distraction of sight, smells and sounds were magnified. Sometimes he even shut his eyes as he followed the huge gray bulk of his mother and let the sea fill him with its sensory symphony. He felt the increasing coolness of the water and tasted the pungent richness of the fertile waters. But most of all, he sensed his mother's urgency to reach their destination. Northward. Northward. Northward!

Chapter 21

Payoff Rendezvous

Saturday May 4th, 12:30 a.m.
Just north of Newport

A moonlit night. Perfect time for a hunt. Possibly his last one of the voyage. Carefully, Freddie kneeled and pulled his rifle out of his trunk. Loading it was second nature to him now. He slung the weapon under his arm and cautiously climbed the stairs to the deck. Not a soul around. Just the rhythmic up and down motion of the ship as they sailed south. He glanced up at the wheelhouse. The light was on, but he couldn't see anyone.

Freddie crept around behind a bulkhead and knelt down. He had a perfect view of the water, and the moon's iridescent light spread across the water's surface. There! Off to the bow were ripples and a tail just disappearing. Any second now, they should be exactly opposite the northbound creature.

He jumped as two whales blew noisily not ten yards away. A mother and a baby. As the mother whale's broad back exposed itself above the surface, Freddie pulled the rifle close to him, sighted through the scope, and squeezed the trigger. A hit — he was sure of it.

* * *

Saturday, May 4th, 1 a.m.
Newport, Oregon

"Can't this wait until tomorrow?" Les complained as they drove toward the hidden beach south of the cave. "I mean, like we haven't had any sleep in 24 hours."

"You mean, I haven't had any sleep. You guys snored most of the way home. We've got to retrieve the stuff tonight. After we get the money from Freddie tomorrow, we'll take right off for Yakima. Make the delivery just after dark. Then I promise you, we can loll around for a couple of days before we come back. Maybe you can even pick up some more cowboy duds."

Dirk grunted.

"Well, you'd better let one of us drive up there then. You're going to fall asleep over the wheel."

"No, I won't fall asleep," George said quietly. "Now let's get on with this — make the pickup so we can get back to the motel and sleep some before it's time to meet Freddie."

They hid the truck under some trees and changed into wetsuits. Keeping a watchful eye on the road, the three men, carrying their boat, slipped across the highway and down the embankment.

"At least the water's calmer than on the last pickup," Les said.

"Yeah, and no moonlight. We won't be as visible. This should be a piece of cake," said George. "Let's do it."

They put into the water and slowly made their way up the coastline to the entrance of the cave. This time, George held the boat steady while Les and Dirk swam in to get the bundles. They were back in less than five minutes.

"What's the matter?" George shouted as they came out empty-handed.

"Gone! The stuff's all gone!"

In a flash, George was over the side of the boat. Les reached out and caught the rope on the front just as the boat started to drift away. He handed his underwater flashlight to George.

Quickly, Dirk and George swam back into the cave. The water depth was about four feet at the back. They stood up, their voices echoing over the waves sloshing against the rock walls of the wet cavern.

"Did you look on the bottom? Maybe the stuff fell off."

"No, Boss. Remember, we tied all those bundles."

Frantically, George ran his hand along the ledge where they had stored the kilos.

"Look at this!"

He aimed his flashlight at a cut piece of twine he grasped in his fingers. One end was still attached to the rock outcropping.

"Somebody's taken it."

"Let's get out of here," Les urged.

"Not until I make sure," George said as he submerged himself to search the rocky floor of the cave.

Nervously, Les waited, edging toward the entrance.

"Hurry up; let's go," Dirk yelled to George as he came to the surface.

Les slithered over the side of the boat just ahead of George. Dirk gunned the outboard motor, and soon they were racing back to the beach. No one said a word as they got out and scrambled back up the trail to the top and then ran for the cover of the trees.

"Come on, come on," George hissed as they peeled off their wetsuits and clambered back into their clothes.

The men climbed back in the truck, shivering from the cold and nervousness as George eased the truck out onto the highway.

"Where to now?" Dirk asked as they headed south of town.

"Well, definitely not back to our old place. Someone may be watching it. Let's go down near Yachats and camp out on a logging road."

"Camp?"

"Well, what do you suggest? We don't know who picked that stuff up. There may be cops looking for us right now. If it weren't for the fact we haven't been paid, we'd be on our way to another state. But I'm going to meet with Freddie tomorrow no matter what. So we'll just have to lay low until then."

"But if someone had seen us, don't you suppose we'd be arrested by now? Think about it, Boss," Dirk said.

"You may be right, but I'm not taking any chances."

"Someone did see us," Les said as they sped along the coast highway. "Remember that girl, Thursday night? The one up on the bluff?"

"Aw, she couldn't know who we are."

They reached the logging road and bounced along it until they were deep in the cover of the woods.

"You and Les get in the back; I'll sleep up here," George told them.

"Man, we're gonna freeze."

"Put some of those burlap bags over you or your wetsuits. You'll survive."

Muttering under their breath, the two men reluctantly climbed out of the cab and opened the canopy so they could get in the back. The truck jostled back and forth as they tried to arrange themselves for the night.

George rolled a towel up under his head and lay down on the seat. He was still cold from the water, but part of his trembling was from the thoughts going through his mind. Thoughts of the meeting with Freddie in which he would tell him that they'd lost the drugs.

What were the chances of Freddie paying him for the last shipment after this? George knew very little of the chain of command to which Freddie reported, but he supposed there would be someone out to get Freddie's hide if the drugs weren't delivered. Would that someone be after them too? Probably.

"How stupid can I be?" he said aloud to himself. "I don't have to tell Freddie anything. We'll just take the money and disappear. At least, I will. If those yokels don't, tough luck."

He thought about the money he had secreted away in a bank account. Maybe he shouldn't even risk a meeting with Freddie — just abandon the truck and walk into town and catch a bus to somewhere. Somewhere far away. His stomach churned as he considered his unappealing options.

The jostling and voices in the back quieted down. George lay still, staring at the blackness of night through the windshield. If he didn't get paid, what would Les and Dirk do? Kill him? He wouldn't put it past them. He had to get that payment from Freddie, no matter what. He could worry about the future later.

The stress of the last 24 hours of wakefulness overtook him, and he fell asleep. The next thing he knew Les was shaking him awake.

"Hey Boss, I hear logging trucks. I think we'd better get out of here."

George sat up with a start. Seven o'clock. Bright sunlight flooded the cab. With a rush, the night came back to him. Well, so much for running off now.

"Okay, okay. Just let me sit up."

Dirk and Les climbed in the cab with him, and George started the engine. They waited while a logging truck drove past them on the road. When it was gone, they pulled out from behind the cover of the trees and drove down the road to the coast highway.

"Is Freddie going to call you?"

"Yeah, but I think he'll show up at the cafe where we usually meet anyway."

They stopped at a rest stop and cleaned up in the bathroom. George put the change he had left into the concession machines and got them each a Coke and candy bar for breakfast. As they ate, he gave them directions.

"Okay — at 9:30, you drop me off near Old Town. Then just keep driving — go inland — park the truck somewhere where you can't be seen. At 11:00, come back. I'll be up at the top of the hill."

They waited for another hour, just sitting in the truck behind a warehouse south of town. Then George got out and changed positions with Dirk. Slowly, they drove across the bridge into town.

"I've got an idea," said Dirk.

"What's that?" George asked.

"I'll tell you after you come back with the money."

George looked at him, surprised. Usually he was the one with the ideas. And he wasn't used to Dirk or Les giving him instructions. But now didn't seem to be the time for arguing. It was 9:30. Dirk let him out at the top of the hill that led down to Old Town.

It was cloudy and slightly chilly, so the usual tourists weren't out like they were on most Saturday mornings. George made his way casually down the hill, trying to look like a local just out for a walk. A couple of people even smiled and half-waved to him, so by the time he approached the wharf, he felt almost confident.

The Coffee Cup Cafe was open as usual. George ordered a big steaming mug of coffee and slid into a vacant booth at the end. He hadn't been there five minutes before Freddie joined him. He was carrying a knapsack that he tucked under the table before sitting down.

"Everything okay?" Freddie questioned.

"Yeah. Why?"

"You just look sort of tired."

"Well, we had a late delivery last night."

"Why weren't you at the motel when I called?"

"We moved to another place," George lied. "I wanted a place that wasn't right on the highway."

"Have you given your contacts the new number?"

"Yeah. Here it is."

George made up a number, scrawled it on a napkin, and pushed it across the table toward Freddie.

"The boss is pleased," said Freddie.

"Good."

"There may be three more runs this year. If you guys keep on doing what you're doing, you might get a raise."

"Great."

Freddie looked at George curiously. There was something he wasn't telling him.

"You're sure everything's going okay?"

"Yeah."

Freddie eyed him suspiciously and then looked at the phone number again. Without a word, he got up, carrying the knapsack with him, and walked over to a pay phone. George sat at the table nervously fiddling with his coffee cup. In a couple of minutes, Freddie returned.

"Let's go," he said, laying money for the coffee on the table.

George followed him, frantically trying to decide what to do. Freddie steered him toward a line of shrubs at the back of the parking lot and motioned for George to follow. There was no one around and Freddie brought his face up close to George's.

"That's not a real number — what's going on?" he hissed.

George stared at the ground. Freddie quietly put his hand in his pocket.

"I said what's going on?"

"The drugs are gone," George mumbled. "Someone stole them from the cave."

He waited, wondering if Freddie would just shoot him there.

"Who took them — police?"

"No, we think a college girl did."

"A girl?"

"Yeah, a girl. We saw her and a guy when we stowed them last time."

"Where are your buddies?"

"Probably waiting up on the highway for me."

"Come on," Freddie said roughly as he pushed George toward the sidewalk. "We need to have a serious talk."

They got to the highway in two minutes just as Dirk and Les came by. They pulled over to the side, looking curiously at Freddie.

"Get in the back," George motioned to Les.

Dirk and Les exchanged frightened glances, but Les obediently got out and climbed in through the back canopy.

Freddie and George got in the front seat.

"Where are you staying?" Freddie asked.

"I'm not sure — we're afraid to go back to the old place in case it's staked out."

"Just find a place out of town — we've got a lot of talking to do," Freddie commanded.

Dirk drove north through town and then headed east toward the valley. "Where should I go?" Dirk asked as they made the cutoff north toward Portland.

"Find a motel," Freddie commanded.

"Then you don't think our pictures are plastered on the front page — that's what you were saying last night," Dirk said to George, ignoring Freddie.

George held up a copy of the Newport paper.

"There's nothing in here about us or the drugs."

144

They drove for about ten miles and then stopped at the Sleepy Hollow cabins next to a small grocery store. Dirk parked the truck in back while George checked them in. Les and Dirk followed Freddie warily into the motel. No introductions had been made, but it was obvious who he was and even more obvious that George had spilled the beans to him.

They sat down in the motel, George and Freddie on corner chairs and Les and Dirk stiffly on the edge of the beds.

"Tell me about this girl," Freddie said.

"She works at the Marine Science Center," Les volunteered. "She's seen us a couple of times. We chased her once just for fun."

"You idiots." Freddie shook his head in disgust. "You sure the cops aren't involved?"

"If the cops found the stuff, don't you think there'd be something in the paper about it?" Dirk asked.

"Yeah," mumbled Les.

George raised his eyebrows, listening with interest to this conversation.

"But if someone else took it — say someone who wanted to sell it — then what?" Dirk said.

"Get to the point, Dirk," George said.

"Well, little Miss Ponytail is college age — right? She's at the Marine Science Center so she probably either works there or is a student there."

"Go on," George said. "I don't know anything about the place."

"Well I do. So maybe she and that guy she was with saw us coming out of the cave and decided to investigate. And being bright kids, they realized that what they'd found wasn't just chalk dust."

"What would they do with it?"

"That's just the point. Probably nothing. Maybe they've got a couple of friends who sniff coke, but they don't know anything about dealing. But they do know enough to realize they've got something valuable — really valuable."

"And?"

"If that's the case, then she's probably got the stuff right with her. Probably sitting in her closet while she decides what to do with it."

"I think you're crazy, Dirk," George said.

"I don't," Freddie said quietly.

"You willing to walk away from this kind of money if there's even a chance I'm right — a chance we could get the stuff back and be in business again?"

"Well I guess it wouldn't hurt to look."

"I say we pay Little Miss Ponytail a social call," said Dirk.

"When?"

"Tonight."

"My ship doesn't sail until tomorrow morning," Freddie said. "So I'm going with you. You'd better hope she has the drugs and that you get them back. Or you're in bigger trouble than you realize."

The men looked at him and then stared at the floor.

Chapter 22

Bertha

Saturday May 4th, 10 p.m.
Marine Science Center

"**K**A7ITR from KA7SJP. Go ahead, Marc." Kim lay on her bed, the coax connecting her two-meter rig to the outside antenna, draped across her feet. She plumped a pillow under her head and settled back for an enjoyable good-night QSO with Marc.

"So what did you do today, Kim? Any more excitement?"

"No, thank goodness. I spent the whole day studying like a good girl. I think I may be almost caught up by the time Monday rolls around. How about you? Did you fix the repeater?"

"Yeah, we did. Some mice had built a nest in it and chewed through some of the cable. Luckily, we had nice weather. How's it over there?"

"Incredible. It was cloudy and cool this morning, and then all of a sudden, it warmed up about twenty degrees this afternoon. Feels like July. I've still got the windows open. And I guess it's supposed to be sunny the rest of the week and around eighty degrees."

"That's especially nice for the coast."

"Yeah, maybe I'll go surfing."

"Kim..."

"Just kidding, Marc."

"Have you got the whale's head working okay?"

"Yeah, I just tested everything except the fire extinguisher after dinner. Works great. I can hardly wait for tomorrow night. One thing worries me though. I'm not sure how far that fire extinguisher will shoot. Guess we better have Dr. Bolny stand well back in the hall until that part is over."

"Good idea. Wish I could be there. Remember everything just as it happens so you can tell me."

"I promise."

They chatted a few minutes more and then signed with their customary "88's" (love and kisses). Kim stretched and sat up to look out the window. She was still dressed in her jeans and sweatshirt and tennis shoes. She supposed she should get ready for bed, but somehow she wasn't sleepy. After the excitement of the weekend and her happiness at being reunited with Marc, she felt almost giddy.

"Look at that moon," she whispered, peeking out the kitchen window.

The salty scent of the ocean air wafted in through the window, beckoning her. Kim grabbed a lightweight jacket and put the portable antenna on her small two-meter rig before slipping it in her pocket. Her other two-meter transceiver was hooked up to Bertha, waiting for the party.

"Just a short walk," she said aloud to herself. "Then some hot chocolate, and maybe I can sleep."

Kim let herself out of the apartment. Her footsteps echoed as she made her way down the metal steps that led to the courtyard. The deserted Marine Science Center seemed almost eerie in the moonlight shadows. She walked by the metal sculpture of three seals sitting on a rock and hurried through the archway. In the distance, she thought she could hear a high screeching sound.

"Hi Muriel," Kim giggled, remembering Jack's ghost story.

Beyond the courtyard, Kim walked briskly toward the parking lot. No ghost wails now — just the surf and the occasional tooting of a foghorn. It was a beautiful night. She wished Marc were here to walk on the beach with her. Maybe he would be able to come back again before the term was over.

Out in the fresh air, Kim felt her fatigue from studying fall away. She started walking faster and faster until she was jogging toward the beach. With the moon and the stars and the ocean as her companions, she thought about the migrating whales and wondered if they noticed the wonder of a night like this.

* * *

11:30

"Over there — in the back of the lot."

"Where does she live?"

"Probably in the back. I think the students have apartments there. But it doesn't look like there's a soul here. Not a single car. She's probably gone too."

"All the better. We can search her apartment without anyone knowing."

"How will we find hers?"

"Look on mailboxes."

Dirk whistled in surprise.

"Won't have to — looks like there is someone home after all."

The men followed his pointing finger. At the far end of the lot, a lone figure was jogging up the pathway. There was no mistaking the curly pony-tail that swung behind her.

"Look — she's going in there between the buildings. Let her get up close to her place and then we'll grab her. Make sure you cover her mouth — just in case there is anyone else here," Freddie ordered.

In a flash, the four men were away from the side of the truck where they had been standing, and running in the darkness along the building. Kim paused under the covered walkway to catch her breath. The men flattened out against the wall, waiting for her to move.

She stretched her arms and then stopped, putting one leg up on a bench to cool down her muscles. She had just put that leg down and was putting the other one up, when she turned her head, looking back through the entryway.

It was obvious she sensed something. Her whole posture stiffened as she slowly put her leg down and pulled her radio from her belt while moving backward, her eyes riveted on the corner of the building where the four men hid.

"Get her!" whispered Les.

Like panthers they sprang, pounding across the court-yard.

Kim froze for just an instant and then began running, screaming for help as she raced across the courtyard.

She pulled a key from her pocket as she ran. Instantly she realized it was the key to the lab, not her apartment. But in that same flash, she saw that she was right next to the door that led to the labs — and her apartment was farther away.

She jammed the key into the lock and shoved the hall door open. One of the men grabbed the door just as she was slamming it behind her. With furious strength, she pulled it closed and twisted the lock.

Desperate to escape, she ran down the hall. There were yells and shattering glass behind her as she pounded down the hall, around the corner, and grabbed the doorknob to the bone lab. It was unlocked. She ducked inside and pushed the lock button.

She could hear them running down the hall.

"Over here!" one of them yelled as footsteps approached the door.

Crawling on her hands and knees, Kim scooted across the floor around Bertha and hid under a table. The noise of her own breathing seemed to fill the room. A phone was ten feet away on a table. She heard a door across the hall crash open. Flattening herself against the wall, Kim pulled her radio from her coat. She was trembling so badly, it was hard to make her hands cooperate.

This will have to work, she thought frantically as she punched up the repeater and called 911.

Even before the emergency operator could answer, a voice came back to her on the repeater.

"Kim, are you all right? This is Gary."

"Newport Dispatch. What is your emergency?"

Kim told them both at the same time.

"Send help," she said breathlessly. "To the Marine Science Center — I'm in the bone lab, Gary. The drug guys are here."

Now they were working on the door next to hers. And then suddenly the wood on the bone lab door was splintering as the men kicked it repeatedly. Kim crouched further back under the table. In the next instant, she knew they would turn on the light and then it would all be over. The men hammered on the door with something hard. A board broke and the hall light shone in through the hole. She held her breath as a hand reached through and grabbed the doorknob.

Light reflected off the huge skull of Bertha that Kim had dragged across the floor so that it was in line with the door. Instantly, she knew what she had to do.

Saying a prayer, she aimed the antenna of her two-meter rig at the Dual Tone Multi Function decoder apparatus she had attached inside the skull. The door was opening very slowly. She could see the silhouette of a man in the doorway, a gun in his raised hand.

Now! Even in the dark, she knew the positions on her tone pad by heart. She depressed number one. A huge spray of carbon dioxide vapor shot out of the whale's mouth, blasting the man back from the doorway.

Number Two. She hit the button. Even while the fire extinguisher was still going, the tape loop started. Another man appeared and then froze as the sound of the tape loop began — "I am the voice of dead whales..." For a second, she saw two more male figures in front of the open door. Kim hit number four — flashing red strobe lights in Bertha's eyes, and then she punched number five. The loud wailing siren of the car alarm shrieked through the building.

For several anxious minutes, Kim hid under the table. The noise of the alarm with all its various pitches and tempos was deafening. She waited for what seemed like an eternity as the alarm went through its routine. Then it was silent. Shivering from fright, Kim sat motionless, listening to the empty hallway. Suddenly, the light in the room snapped on.

"Kim?"

She looked up to see Gary's reassuring face. The alarm had started over again and she crawled over to unplug the decoder from Bertha.

"I'm here," she said weakly.

Gary reached down and pulled her to her feet with strong hands.

"You okay?"

"Yeah. The guys we saw — they were here."

"I know. The police are chasing them right now. They were zooming out of the parking lot when we got here. I was more concerned about you."

He paused and bent over to look at the devices attached to Bertha.

"Looks like you had quite a reception for them."

"This was..."

Kim stopped, suddenly laughing and crying at the same time.

"I know this sounds strange...but this was supposed to be a birthday surprise party for Dr. Bolny."

Gary examined the various devices Kim had hooked into the whale's head. Then he put his arm around Kim.

"Best birthday present, I've ever seen. And I bet Dr. Bolny will think so too when he finds out it saved you."

"Why did they come after me?"

"Let's go find out."

They walked out to the parking lot. Two police cars with their lights still flashing were over at the access road. The officers stooped over three men lying face down on the ground, handcuffed.

Gary took Kim's hand and they walked over. Captain Stills was panting after their struggle.

"Are these the men you saw before in town?" he asked her, shining a flashlight on George, Les, and Dirk.

Kim looked at them and involuntarily shuddered.

"Yes, but I think there was another one in the building too."

"These three were in the truck," Captain Stills said.

"You got something that belongs to us," Dirk snarled at her, trying to raise his upper body.

Captain Stills pushed him back on the ground. Kim turned away and went over to stand by Gary.

"Is that why they came here? They think I have the drugs with me?"

"I gather that's what they were thinking," Gary said.

"So where did the drugs come from?"

"We don't know," Captain Stills said. "So far none of them seems inclined to give us that information. Maybe that will change when we get down to the station."

Gary glanced around at the empty parking lot as the police cars left.

"Are you the only one here?"

"I guess so," Kim said. "But there'll be some people back in the morning plus the staff who run the exhibits and the gift store."

"Come on, you're going to spend the night at our house. I don't think you've ever met my wife, Amy, and our two-year-old, Shannon."

"Oh really, Gary. I'm okay here."

"No, that's a Coast Guard order — go get your stuff."

Kim smiled and snapped a weak salute. Secretly she was glad for the invitation. She ran to her room and grabbed a few things and came back.

"Only thing I didn't tell you is that our cat climbs into bed with any visiting guests," Gary told her as they climbed into his car.

"Great. I miss my cat, Daisy. This will be just like being home."

* * *

Saturday, May 4th, midnight
Newport

Freddie crouched under the bridge abutment and waited until the police cars left. The voice of the whale's skull was still in his brain ..."I am the voice of dead whales." He shook his head from side to side, trying to clear away the image of the gleaming red eyes.

His knees folded under him and he sat down on the cold ground, leaning up against the concrete pillar. He had to get away. The *Si Maria* was in port — he guessed a couple of miles away by foot. He waited until his shaking stopped and then furtively began jogging alongside the road. The bridge was the most dangerous part. Shoving his hands in his pockets and keeping his head down, he walked across, fighting the impulse to drop to the pavement every time a car passed. On the other side, he stopped to rest a few minutes and then resumed his trek back to the ship.

No one was awake when he slipped aboard at 3 a.m. Quietly, he got into his bunk and lay still, staring into the darkness. Thoughts of the lost drugs and what would happen when he returned to Colombia swirled through his head. He tried closing his eyes, but then the red glowing eyes of the whale pierced into him.

Half sobbing, he turned on his side and waited for morning.

Chapter 23

Shot in the Dark

Sunday, May 5th
Newport

As soon as they were done with breakfast, Kim thanked Gary and his wife and asked to be taken back to the Marine Science Center. Gary dropped her off on his way to work.

"So what happens now?" Kim asked. "How will they find out where those drugs came from?"

"Captain Stills is working the waterfront right now. He has photos of the three men and is asking everyone for information. Just be patient — something will turn up. Those guys didn't strike me as bright enough to be doing this thing on their own. Someone must be supplying."

Gary seemed a little worried about her going back to the Marine Science Center, but when they drove in the parking lot, there were already several cars there. Some of the students and staff had come back early from the conference. Kim thanked him and carried her stuff to her apartment. Julia and Megan weren't home yet.

She went down to the building that housed the labs to see how badly things were damaged. The maintenance crew had been called early this morning, and they were hard at work trying to patch up the doors that had been broken through.

"Wow, Kim," Jeff the head custodian greeted her as he removed what was left of the entryway door. "I've heard part of the story, but not all of it. Looks like there was a real battle here."

Kim helped him pick up the pieces of splintered wood and glass from the floor.

"Yeah — I really caused a mess, didn't I? I sure didn't mean to."

As they swept the hall together, she told him the details of the night before.

"Well, as long as you're okay, that's all that matters," Jeff reassured her. "We'll get a carpenter in here first thing tomorrow to fix this all up. Right now, I'm just going to put plastic over the holes to keep the wind out."

Kim walked down the hall to the bone lab. Debris from the broken door was all over the floor. She grabbed a broom and began sweeping.

When she was done restoring the room to order, just for fun, she plugged the decoder back in and pushed number two on her handheld. Sure enough, the birthday greeting on the tape loop started. The eyes also worked. She didn't try the confetti or the alarm. She wasn't quite sure what Dr. Bolny's reaction to all this would be. She was probably the first student at the center to run up a repair bill like this. Not exactly a great birthday present for him.

She gathered up some of her notebooks and took them to her room. The phone was ringing as she entered the door.

It was Captain Stills asking her to come down to the station later on and fill out some more paperwork.

"Sure. Have you found out anything more?"

"Possibly. Someone in a cafe definitely recognized one of the men. Said he saw him having coffee last week with a guy carrying a satchel, and he thinks the guy was a crewman from one of the foreign vessels in port. We're trying to track down exactly what ships were in that day. Then we'll call Portland to get the crew list."

* * *

1 p.m.

Back at the police station, DEA officers were busy questioning Dirk, Les and George separately. After two hours, it was pretty obvious that George wasn't going to talk. There seemed to be someone or something that he feared more than the jail sentence he was now facing. Les was also uncooperative. But Dirk was another story.

When told the possible sentences he faced for his involvement, and also told that they might be lighter if he cooperated, he agreed to tell them what he knew. Someone named Freddie aboard the *Si Maria* was the supplier. Yes, he had been with them the night before, and yes, he had gotten away.

No, he didn't know where the ship was now. No, he didn't know who was Freddie's boss. He didn't even know the ship's country of origin. George had told Dirk and Les as little as possible. The officers locked Les up and went back to question George. Meanwhile a call went out to the Coast Guard to locate the *Si Maria*.

* * *

3 p.m.

"N7UXP from AA7NC."

"Go ahead AA7NC."

"Hey, do you have another phone number for KA7SJP? I have a message for her. Looked her up on my Sam Data Base but there's no answer at this number."

"AA7NC, this is KC7YN. Kim's at the Oregon State Marine Science Center this term."

Kim dropped the dustrag she had been wiping off the table with and scurried over to her rig. She had turned on two meters just to monitor while she worked tidying up the apartment.

"AA7NC, this is KA7SJP. Go ahead."

"Hi Kim. There's a W6POE on twenty meters right now looking for you. He heard your bulletin on the maritime net and wants to talk to you. He's right around 14.240."

"Okay. Thank you very much. I'm going there right now. AA7NC from KA7SJP clear."

She turned on her low-band rig and tuned up twenty meters.

"W6POE from KA7SJP."

"KA7SJP from W6POE. His signal was a little weak but readable.

"Go ahead W6POE."

"Kim, I heard your bulletin last week to maritime users. I'm currently on a fishing vacation with some friends and we're about ten miles north of Reedsport. But two nights ago we were up above Newport. Around midnight, we were sitting on the deck, just chatting and saw what looked like gunfire coming from a steamer about a mile away. Couldn't really hear anything, but I remembered what you asked people to look for. Probably five or six shots."

"Any idea of the name of the ship?"

"No — couldn't see it, but it was heading south. We got out binoculars — pretty good light that night. I would guess it was maybe hauling lumber. Definitely heading south."

"KA7SJP from KC7YN."

Kim turned back to her two-meter rig.

"Go ahead KC7YN."

"Kim, I'm monitoring on twenty. Can't really hear you because you're so close but I can hear the other station. Did he say the ship was heading south?"

"Yes, he did."

"I was just talking to my old friend W7RXJ in Coos Bay. He'll pass this information on to the club there and down the coast. Sooner or later, we'll catch this guy."

Kim thanked all the hams and signed. She picked up the phone to call the Coast Guard and then hesitated. With the drug mystery in front of them, would they even be interested in who was shooting whales?

She dialed and asked for Gary.

"Kim! I was just going to call you. You were definitely right about there being a fourth guy last night. The guy's name is Freddie and he's aboard the *Si Maria*. I'm hoping the authorities are arresting him in Coos Bay now as we speak."

"Did the other guys confess?"

"Just one of them at first, but now they're all talking. I'll have more to tell you later."

"Gary, believe it or not, the real reason I called is about something else. I know this may not seem as important as what happened last night, but I just got a lead on who may be shooting those gray whales. Someone saw the gunfire coming from a lumber freighter two nights ago north of Newport."

Gary sighed.

"Yeah, you're right. We've kind of got our hands full but give me the information anyway. We'll certainly check on it."

"All I know is that it's a lumber freighter and it's headed south."

"Lumber freighter? I wonder. No, that would be too much of a coincidence."

"What are you talking about, Gary?"

"Let me call you back later."

Kim held the receiver in her hand even after Gary had hung up.

*　*　*

7 p.m.

"He's coming," Florence told Kim over the phone. "His wife just phoned and they were on their way. I've got the cake ready — what do you want me to do?"

"Just lead him to the lounge. We'll keep the cake hidden until after the surprise."

Kim, Megan and Julia along with Chris and half a dozen other students ran down the hall to the lounge where they planned on hiding behind a couch in one corner. At Kim's urging, Bertha had been moved to the lounge.

"I know he thinks he's coming down here to see the damage, and he will, but first it'd be nice to wish him Happy Birthday in a room that still has intact doors."

Kim smiled ruefully. The other students had been teasing her all afternoon about her adventure and the havoc she had wreaked on the lab area. But mostly, they had been supportive and grateful that she hadn't been hurt.

It was all she could do to get through the afternoon, knowing that as she scurried around arranging things that the man who had murdered the whales might be being apprehended. And what of the drug dealers? What did Gary mean by something being a coincidence? He had refused to tell her more and she was reluctant to call him back.

At four, she phoned Marc and brought him up to date. She mentioned the calls of all the hams she had talked to.

"Hey, I know W7RXJ. He's on Packet (computer message system transmitted by Amateur Radio). Let me send him a message right now and see if anything's happening in the bay. Why don't you monitor two meters for me?"

"Marc, it would be better if we set a schedule. How about five? I have to help arrange things downstairs."

At five, Kim ran back to the apartment.

"KA7ITR from KA7SJP."

"Here's KA7ITR. Hi Kim. I have some news."

"Well what is it?"

Kim twisted the microphone cord anxiously as she waited for his reply.

"The Coast Guard arrested someone from the *Si Maria*. That's all my friend knew. He saw them go aboard and about thirty minutes later, they came out leading a guy. He was taken away by local police."

"Oh. Marc. I just have to know. I think I'll try to call Gary at the station."

"Good idea. I'll stand by."

She was back in a minute.

"He's not there. The man who answered said he was out on business and wouldn't be back until later tonight. I guess we'll just have to wait."

"Kim, when can you call me back?"

"Well, we're having that party tonight, so I don't know. At ten for sure, but if I hear anything earlier, I'll give you a call. Leave your rig on."

They signed and Kim ran back downstairs to help rearrange the furniture in the lounge so they could all fit behind it. She did a trial test of Bertha. Perfect. She had just gone back to the apartment to try and call Gary again when Florence phoned. She ran to tell the others.

Giggling, the students crouched down behind the couch. Kim knelt beside the couch, her two-meter transceiver in hand with its antenna pointed at Bertha. The room was in total darkness while they waited for Dr. Bolny.

"So why are we going down here if all the damage is over in the labs?" they heard him say.

"Just a minute dear," came his wife's reply. "There's something here you should see first."

Someone coughed behind Kim and she said "shhh" quietly as the Bolnys came to the doorway. Kim waited until she saw them. In fact, Dr. Bolny was just reaching inside to turn on the room light when Kim hit the number two button.

"Greetings!" the voice began. "Greetings from the land of dead whales."

She activated the red strobe lights.

"What the?" he exclaimed as Kim started the siren. He flipped on the light switch just as she pushed number three. The untested confetti drop worked perfectly, and a cascade of brightly colored paper floated down on the professor's head as the students jumped to their feet and shouted "Happy Birthday!"

Dr. Bolny stood still with a look of amazement on his face. Then he began laughing.

"So was all this stuff about Kim and drug smugglers chasing her just a hoax to get me down here?"

"No, I'm afraid that part is all true," said Kim coming forward. "But we wanted to have the party for you anyway."

Just then, Florence came in bearing the cake laden with fifty candles.

"Fire extinguisher!" Chris yelled.

"I'm afraid I already used that," Kim said.

They were cutting the cake and pouring sparkling cider when Dr. Bolny gave a puzzled look toward the doorway. Captain Stills and Gary, both in uniform, and both looking very official were standing there. Kim walked over to them.

"What happened?"

"Lots. You have more than a birthday to celebrate," Gary said to Dr. Bolny who was looking quite perplexed. "This

161

young lady here and a friend of hers discovered some hidden bundles of cocaine north of Newport."

The room was silent as everyone listened.

"As if that weren't enough," Gary continued. "It seems that Kim had alerted the Amateur Radio community to be on the lookout for whoever was killing the gray whales. A tip from a ham told us that he was on a lumber freighter. And guess what the guy was on who was supplying the cocaine to the pickup men here in Newport."

"A lumber freighter," Kim whispered, her mouth dropping open in surprise.

Captain Stills laughed at the expression on Kim's face.

"Exactly — Gary here began to put two and two together. When the authorities arrested him on the *Si Maria* in Coos Bay, they searched his cabin and found a rifle with a silencer on it. They questioned the crew and it seems all of them knew the guy shot at something at night. I'm pretty sure we have our man. Not a nice person in any sense of the word, Kim. But he's in custody now, and the guys who chased you have decided they're willing to talk. I think we're going to get names and addresses of every one of their customers."

"And there won't be any more dead whales?"

"Not by this guy."

"That's the best birthday present I could receive," Dr. Bolny said as everyone applauded.

* * *

10 p.m.

"You should have been here, Marc. Without you, none of this would have happened. I mean, it was your idea to go into the cave."

They talked for thirty minutes, pausing every few to ask if anyone wanted to use the repeater. But if there were hams listening, they were only too happy to allow them the frequency.

"Does this mean you want to be a marine biologist, Kim?"

162

"I'm not sure, Marc. Not sure about very many things except one."

"What's that Kim?"

"I can't tell you on the air, silly. There may be people listening. How about in person next weekend."

Marc laughed and then quietly said, "88's Kim. I can hardly wait."

"88's Marc."

Chapter 24

Freedom from Fear

Sunday May 12th — midnight
West of Vancouver Island
British Columbia

S ilver Star broke the water's surface. The tang of fir trees and the rich pungency of oyster beds filled the night spring air. He inhaled deeply, savoring the new smells, before plunging beneath the dark Pacific Ocean.

Finally, his mother had slowed to normal speed. For the first day after she was struck by Freddie's bullet, she had been almost frenzied in her effort to move northward. Only Silver Star's panicked calls had kept her from moving out of his range completely.

Silver Star still remembered the taste of his mother's blood in the water. He had no idea what had happened — just that there had been a loud noise and then his mother jerked and dove straight to the bottom. He had hovered near the surface, waiting for her return. When she came back up, she was far ahead of him.

He kept calling her and gradually the distance between them closed. "Swim faster, swim faster" her body language told him. Over the days of the past week, her panic seemed to lessen. Now they were moving along at normal speed. Soon, the incident would fade entirely from Silver Star's young mind.

The superficial wound caused by the bullet, which ripped through the top of his mother's back would heal completely, leaving her with a white scar that would cause fishermen to nickname her "Stripe." The wound to her memory would remain forever.

In the years to come, she would always be wary of man, and she would pass that fear on to her young. She would never understand that most of mankind was working hard to protect her species and keep the waters safe for future generations.

But for now, the water was cold and rich and peaceful. The Arctic beckoned her to return to continue the life cycle. She paused for Silver Star to nurse and then thrust her body forward again. They would be home soon.

Author's Note

Spring in Oregon brings not only daffodils and tulips, but also the northward migration of the gray whale. It was my privilege this year to be trained as a volunteer whale watcher at the Oregon State University Hatfield Marine Science Center in Newport, Oregon. As I stood on the coastal bluffs helping visitors to spot the magnificent whales, I could only hope that the future relationship between men and whales will be brighter than it has been in the past.

Easy Target is the story of the vulnerability of both man and animal to those who take aim — whether it be with a high-powered rifle or a kilo of cocaine. I have combined these serious issues with what I hope is a fun-to-read adventure story and, of course, with my favorite hobby: Amateur Radio.

If there is ever a QSO with a whale, I hope to be the first! In the meantime, I hope to talk to many more of you.

My heartfelt thanks to the following individuals for their technical expertise and encouragement:

Don Giles, Hatfield Marine Science Center

Lenore Jensen, W6NAZ (Lenore read the first chapters of this book before she passed away in May of 1993. As always, she gave me her steadfast support)

Steve Jensen, W6RHM (my brother, the genius)

Bev Lund, Hatfield Marine Science Center

Dr. Bruce Mate, Hatfield Marine Science Center

Hollie Molesworth, KA7SJP

Don Myers, Humane Society of the Willamette Valley

Steffie Nelson, KA1IFB, Proofreader

Richard Ritterband, AA6BC

Pamela Rogers, Hatfield Marine Science Center
Chief Warrant Officer John Sitton, U. S. Coast Guard
Charles Smejkal
Students and Staff of Waldo Middle School's Title I Program
Bob Wall
Dave Wall
Michael Wall, KA7ITR
Dr. Lavern Weber, Hatfield Marine Science Center
Mark Wilson, AA2Z, Editor

73,

Cynthia Wall, KA7ITT

Cynthia Wall, KA7ITT